SIX LITTLE BUNKERS
AT COWBOY JACK'S

BY

LAURA LEE HOPE

SIX LITTLE BUNKERS AT COWBOY JACK'S

CHAPTER I

"A THUNDER STROKE"

"Whew!" said Russ Bunker, looking out into the driving rain.

"Whew!" repeated Rose, standing beside him.

"Whew!" said Vi, and "Whew!" echoed Laddie, while Margy added "Whew!"

"W'ew!" lisped Mun Bun last of all, standing on tiptoe to see over the high windowsill. Mun Bun could not quite say the letter "h"; that is why he said "W'ew!"

Such a September rain the six little Bunkers had never seen before, for the very good reason that they had never before been at the seashore during what Daddy Bunker and Captain Ben called "the September equinox."

"That is an awful funny word, anyway," Rose Bunker said.

"What's funny?" Violet asked.

"Can I make a riddle out of it?" added Laddie.

"It is a riddle," replied Rose, quite confidently. "For 'equinox' is just a rain and wind storm."

"That isn't a riddle," said Laddie promptly. "That's the answer to a riddle."

And perhaps it was, even if Rose had the equinox and the equinoctial storms a little mixed in her mind. At any rate, this was a most surprising storm to all the little Bunkers—the wind blew so hard, the rain came in such big gusts, flattening the white-capped waves which they could see, both from Captain Ben's bungalow and from this old house to which they had come to play. And now, as all six peered out of the attic window of the old house, there was an unexpected flash of lightning, followed by a grumble of thunder.

"Oh! just like a bad, bad dog," gasped Vi, not a little frightened by the noise. "I—I am afraid of thunder."

"I'm not," declared Laddie, her twin.

But perhaps, because he was a boy, he thought he must claim more courage than he really felt. At any rate, he winced a little, too, and drew back from the window.

"Maybe we'd better go back to Captain Ben's house—and mother," suggested Margy in a wee small voice.

"W'ew!" lisped Mun Bun, the littlest Bunker, once more, but quite as bravely as before. Like Laddie (whose name really was Fillmore), Mun Bun wished to claim all the courage a boy should show.

"I guess we can't go back while it rains like this," said Russ, the oldest of the six.

"And Captain Ben thought it would maybe clear up and not rain any more, so we came," announced Rose. "Oh! There goes another thunder stroke."

The rumble of thunder seemed nearer.

"I guess," Russ said soberly, "that Norah or Jerry Simms would call this the clearing-up shower."

"But Norah and Jerry Simms aren't here," Vi reminded him. "Are they?"

"That doesn't make any difference. It can be the clearing-up shower of this equinox, just the same."

"Can it?" asked Vi.

She was always asking questions, and she asked so many that it was quite impossible to answer them all, so, for the most part, nobody tried to answer her. And this was one of the times when nobody answered Vi.

"We'd better keep on playing," Rose said, very sensibly. "Then we won't bother 'bout the thunder strokes."

"It is lightning," objected Russ. "I don't mind the thunder. Thunder is only a noise."

"I don't care," said Rose, "it's the thunder that scares you—— Oh! Hear it?"

"Does the thunder hit you?" asked Vi.

"Why, nothing is going to hit us," Russ replied bravely, realizing that he must soothe any fears felt by his younger brothers and sisters. Russ was nine, and Daddy Bunker and mother expected him to set a good example to

Rose and Laddie and Violet and Margy and Munroe Ford Bunker, who, when he was very little, had named himself "Mun Bun."

"Just the same," whispered Rose in a very small voice, and in Russ's ear, "I wish we hadn't come over from Captain Ben's bungalow this morning when it looked like the rain had all stopped."

"Pooh!" said Russ, still bravely, "it thunders over there just as it does here, Rose Bunker."

Of course that was so, and Rose knew it. But nothing seemed quite so bad when daddy and mother were close at hand.

"Let's play again," she said, with a little sigh.

"What'll we play?" asked Violet. "Haven't we played everything there is?"

"I s'pose we have—some time or other," Rose admitted.

"No, we haven't," interposed Russ, who was of an inventive mind. "There are always new plays to make up."

"Just like making up riddles," agreed Laddie. "I guess I could make up a riddle about this old storm—if only the thunder wouldn't make so much noise. I can't think riddles when it thunders."

The thunder seemed to shake the house. The rain dashed against the windows harder than ever. And there were places in the roof of this attic where the water began to trickle through and drop upon the floor.

"Oh!" cried Mun Bun, on whose head a drop fell. "It's leaking! I don't like a leaky house. Let's go home, Rose."

"Do you want to go home to Pineville, Mun Bun?" shouted Russ, for he could not make his voice heard by the others just then without shouting.

"Well, no. But I'd rather be at that other house where mother is—and daddy," proclaimed the smallest boy when the noise of the thunder had again passed.

"I tell you," said Russ soberly, "we'd better go downstairs and play something till the thunder stops."

"What shall we play?" asked Vi again.

"I'll build an automobile and take you all to ride," said the oldest boy confidently.

"Oh, Russ! You can't!" gasped Rose.

"A real automobile like the one that we rode down here in from Pineville?" asked Laddie, opening his eyes very wide.

"Well, no—not just like that," admitted Russ. "But we'll have some fun with it and we won't bother about the thunder."

Rose looked a bit doubtful over that statement. But she knew it was her duty to help the younger children forget their fears. She started down the steep stairs behind Russ. Laddie and Margy came next, while Vi was helping short-legged little Mun Bun to reach the stairway.

And it was just then that the very awful "thunder stroke" came. It seemed to burst right over the roof, and the flash of lightning that came with it almost blinded the children. There was even a smell of sulphur—just like matches. Only it was a bigger smell than any sulphur match could make.

The children's cries were drowned by the crash outside. The lightning had struck a big old tree that overhung the house. The tree trunk was splintered right down from the top, and before the sound of the thunder died away the broken-off part of that tree fell right across the roof.

How the old house shook! Such a ripping and tearing of shingles as there was! Rose could not stifle her shriek. She and Margy and Laddie came tumbling down the rest of the stairs behind Russ.

"Where's Vi and Mun Bun?" demanded the oldest of the six little Bunkers, staring up the dust-filled stairway.

"Oh! Oh! Help me up!" shrieked Vi from the attic.

"Help me!" cried Mun Bun, very much frightened too. "Somebody is holding me down."

"Oh, dear! Oh, dear!" cried Rose, wringing her hands and looking at Russ. "That old roof has fallen in and Vi and Mun Bun are caught under it!"

CHAPTER II

VERY EXCITING NEWS

The old house was still groaning and shaking under the impact of the lightning-smitten tree. It seemed, indeed, as though the whole roof was broken in and that gradually the house must be flattened down into the cellar. Dust and bits of broken wood and plaster were showering down the open stairway.

Although the house might be falling, Russ felt he had to go up those stairs to the aid of the shrieking Vi and Mun Bun. They were both caught under some of the fallen rubbish, and it was Russ Bunker's duty, if nothing more, to aid the younger children.

Russ did not often shirk his duty. Being the oldest of the six Bunker children, he felt his responsibility more than other boys of his age might have done. Anyway, when the others needed help, Russ's first thought was to aid. He was that kind of boy, as all the readers of this series of stories know very well.

Almost always Russ Bunker was not far from a set of carpenter's tools, of which he was very proud, or from other means of "making things." His brothers and sisters thought him quite wonderful when it came to planning new means of amusement and building such things as play automobiles and boats and steam-car trains. It was quite impossible for Russ now, however, to think up any invention that would help his small sister and brother out of their trouble in the attic of the old house. He was quite helpless.

Nine-year-old Russ Bunker was an inventive, cheerful lad, almost always with a merry whistle on his lips, and quite faithful to the trust his parents imposed in him regarding the well-being of his younger brothers and sisters.

With Rose, who was a year younger than Russ, the boy really took much of the care in the daytime of the other little Bunkers. The older ones really had to do this—or else there would have been no fun for any of them. You see, if the older children in a family will not care for the younger, and cheerfully look after them, there can never be so much freedom and fun to enjoy as these six little Bunkers had.

Rose was a particularly helpful little girl, and, being eight years old now, she could assist Mother Bunker a good deal; and she took pride in so doing. That she was afraid of "thunder strokes" must not be counted against her. Ordinarily she made the best of everything and was of a sunny nature.

The twins, Violet and Fillmore, came next in the group of little Bunkers. These two had their own individual natures and could never be overlooked for long in any party. Violet was much given to asking questions, and she asked so many and steadily that scarcely anybody troubled to answer her. Her twin, called Laddie by all, had early made up his mind that the greatest fun in the world was asking and answering riddles.

Margy's real name was Margaret, and, as we have seen, Mun Bun had named himself (just for ordinary purposes) when he was very small. Not that he was very large now, but he could make a tremendous amount of noise when he was—or thought he was—hurt, as he was doing on this very occasion when he and Vi were caught by the crushing-in of the house roof.

After we got acquainted with the Bunker family at home in Pineville, Pennsylvania, they all started on a most wonderful vacation which took them first to the children's mother's mother's house. So, you see, that story is called "Six Little Bunkers at Grandma Bell's."

From that lovely place in Maine the six little Bunkers went to their Aunt Jo's, then to Cousin Tom's, afterward to Grandpa Ford's, then to Uncle Fred's. They had no more than arrived home at Pineville after their fifth series of adventures, than Captain Ben, a distant relative of Mother Bunker's, and recently in the war, came along and took the whole Bunker family down with him to his bungalow at the seashore, the name of that sixth story of the series being "Six Little Bunkers at Captain Ben's."

And the six certainly had had a fine time at Grand View, as the seashore place was called, until this very September day when an equinoctial storm had been blowing for twenty-four hours or more and the lightning-struck tree had fallen upon the roof of the old house in which the six little Bunkers were playing.

But now none of the little Bunkers thought it so much fun—no, indeed! At the rate Vi and Mun Bun were screaming, the accident which held them prisoners in the attic of the old house seemed to threaten dire destruction.

Russ Bunker, when he had recovered his own breath, charged up the dust-filled stairway and reached the attic in a few bounds. But the floor boards were broken at the head of the stairs, and almost the first thing that happened to him when he got up there into the dust and the darkness—yes, and into the rain that drove through the holes in the roof!—was that his head, with an awful "tunk!" came in contact with a broken roof beam.

Russ staggered back, clutching wildly at anything he could lay his hands on, and all but tumbled backwards down the stairs again.

But in clutching for something to break his fall Russ grabbed Vi's curls with one hand. He could not see her in the dark, but he knew those curls very well. And he was bound to recognize Vi when the little girl stammered:

"What's happened? Did the house fall on my legs, Russ? Must you pull my hair off to get me out?"

Mun Bun was bawling all by himself, but near by. He seemed to be quite as immovable as Vi. And perhaps Russ would have been unable to get out either of the unfortunates by himself.

Just then there came a shout of encouragement from outside, and the rapid pounding of feet. The door below burst open and Daddy Bunker's welcome voice cried out:

"Here I am, children! Here I am—and Captain Ben, too! Where are you all?"

In the dusky kitchen it was easy enough to count the three little Bunkers who remained there. But Daddy Bunker was heartily concerned over the absent ones.

"Where are Russ and Vi and Mun Bun?" cried Daddy Bunker.

"They're upstairs—under that old thunder stroke," gasped Margy. "But I guess they're not all dead-ed yet."

"I guess not!" exclaimed Captain Ben, who was a very vigorous young man, being both a soldier and a sailor. "They are all very much alive."

That was proved by the concerted yells of the three in the attic. Both men hurried to mount the stairs. The dust had settled to some degree by this time, and they could see the struggling forms. Russ had almost got Vi loose, and he had not pulled out her hair in doing so.

Daddy Bunker saw that Mun Bun was only caught by his clothing. Captain Ben took Vi from Russ and Daddy Bunker released Mun Bun. Then they all came hurriedly down the stairs.

Mun Bun was still weeping wildly. Laddie looked at him in amazement.

"Why—why," he said, "you're a riddle, Mun Bun."

"I'm not!" sobbed the littlest Bunker.

"Yes, you are," said Laddie. "This is the riddle: Why is Mun Bun like a sprinkling cart?"

"That is too easy!" laughed Captain Ben, setting Vi down on the floor. "It's because Mun Bun scatters water so easily out of his eyes."

They all laughed at that—even Mun Bun himself, only he hiccoughed too. It did not take much to make the children laugh when the danger was over.

"Why did the old thunder stroke have to do that?" asked Vi. "Why did it pin me down across my legs?"

Daddy Bunker hurried them all out of the old house. He was afraid it might fall altogether.

"And then where should we be?" he asked. "I couldn't go away out West to Cowboy Jack's and leave my little Bunkers under that old house, could I?"

At this Russ and Rose immediately began to be excited—only for a reason very different from the effects of the storm. They looked at each other quite knowingly. That was what Daddy Bunker and Mother Bunker were talking about so earnestly the night before!

"Oh, Daddy!" burst out Rose, clinging to his hand, "are you going so far away from us all? Aren't you going to take us to Cowboy Jack's?"

"Why do they call him that?" asked Vi. "Is he part cow and part boy?"

But Daddy Bunker replied to Rose's question quite seriously:

"That is a hard matter to decide. It is a long journey, and you know school will soon begin at Pineville. And you must not miss school."

"But, Daddy," said Russ, very gravely, "you know you take us 'most everywhere you go. It—it wouldn't be fair to Cowboy Jack not to take us to see him, would it?"

Mr. Bunker laughed very much at this suggestion, and hurried them all through the rain toward Captain Ben's bungalow.

CHAPTER III

THE SILVER LINING

One might think that the accident at the old house would have been excitement enough for the six little Bunkers for one forenoon. But Russ and Rose, at least, and soon all the other children, were bubbling with the thought of Daddy Bunker's going West again to look into a big ranch property to which one of his customers had recently fallen heir.

To travel, to see new things, to meet wonderfully nice and kind people, seemed to be the fate of the six little Bunkers. Russ and Rose were sure that no family of brothers and sisters ever had so much fun traveling and so many adventures at the places they traveled to as they did. Russ and Rose were old enough to read about the adventures of other children—I mean children outside of nursery books—and so far the older young Bunkers quite preferred their own good times to any they had ever read about.

"Why!" Russ had once cried confidently, "we have even more fun than Robinson Crusoe and his man Friday. Of course we do."

"Yes. And they had goats," admitted Rose thoughtfully.

The thought of daddy's going away from them, in any case, would have excited the children. But the opening of their school had been postponed for several weeks already, and Russ and Rose, at least, thought they saw the possibility of their father's taking Mother Bunker and all the children with him to the Southwest.

"Only," Russ said gravely, "I don't much care for the name of that man. He sounds like some kind of a foreign man—and you know how those foreign men were that built the railroad down behind our house in Pineville."

"What makes 'em foreign? Their whiskers?" asked Vi, her curiosity at once aroused. "Do all foreigners have whiskers? What makes whiskers grow, anyway? Daddy doesn't have whiskers. Why do other folks?"

"Mother doesn't have whiskers, either," said Margy gravely.

"Say! Why?" repeated Violet insistently.

"Daddy shaves every morning. That is why he doesn't have whiskers," said Rose, trying to pacify the inquisitive Violet.

"Well, does mother shave, too?" immediately demanded Vi. "I never saw her brush. But I've played with daddy's. I painted the front steps with it."

"And you got punished for it, you know," said Russ, grinning at her. "But we were not talking about whiskers—nor shaving brushes."

"Yes we were," said the determined Vi. "I was asking about them."

"Is that man father is going to see an awful foreigner, Russ?" Rose wanted to know.

"I guess not. Father says he's a nice man. He has met him, he says. But his name—oh, it's awful!"

"What is his name?" asked Vi instantly.

If there was a possible chance of crowding in a question, Vi had it on the tip of her tongue to crowd in. This was an hour after the "thunder stroke" had caused such damage to the old house, and Vi was quite her inquisitive little self again.

"His name——" said Russ.

Then he stopped and began to search his pockets. The others waited, but Violet was not content to wait in silence.

"What's the matter, Russ? Do you itch?"

"No, I don't itch," said the boy, with some irritation.

"Well, you act so," said Vi. "What are you doing then, if you're not itching?"

"She means scratching!" exclaimed Rose, but she stared at Russ, too, in some curiosity.

"Oh! I know!" cried Laddie. "It's a riddle."

"What's a riddle?" asked his twin sister eagerly.

"What Russ is doing," said the little boy. "I know that riddle, but I can't just think how it goes. Let's see: 'I went out to the woodpile and got it; when I got into the house I couldn't find it. What was it?'" and Laddie clapped his hands delightedly to think that he had asked a real riddle.

"Oh, I know! I know!" shouted Margy eagerly.

"You do?" asked Laddie. "What is it, then?"

"My Black Dinah dolly that I lost somewhere and we never could find."

"That isn't the whole of that riddle, Laddie," said Russ. "You ought to say: 'And I had it in my hand all the time.' Then you ask 'What was it?'"

"Well, then," said Laddie, rather disappointed to think he had made a mistake in the riddle after all. "What was it, Russ?"

"It was a splinter," said Russ, now drawing a scrap of paper from one pocket. "And here it is——"

"Not the splinter?" gasped Rose.

"No. It was this piece of paper I was hunting for. I wasn't scratching, either. Here it is. This is that foreign man's name."

"What man's name?" asked Vi, who by this time had forgotten what the main subject of the discussion was.

"Cowboy Jack's name!" cried Rose.

"Has he got more names than that?" asked Vi. "Isn't Cowboy Jack enough name for him?"

"His name," said Russ, reading what he had scribbled down on the paper, "is 'Mr. John Scarbontiskil.' That's foreign."

"Oh!" gasped Rose. "I shouldn't think Daddy Bunker would want to go to see a man with a name like that."

"I don't suppose," said Russ, "that he can help his name being that."

"Couldn't he make his own name—and make it a better one?" demanded Vi. "You know, Mun Bun made his name for himself."

"I could not pronounce that name at all," said Rose to Russ. "I guess, after all, maybe we'd better not go to that place."

"What place?"

"Where daddy is going. To that—that Cowboy Jack's place."

"Why not?" asked Russ, almost as promptly as Vi might have asked it had she heard Rose's speech.

"Because," said Rose, who was a thoughtful girl, "of course they don't call him Cowboy Jack to his face, and I should never be able to say Scar—Scar—Scar—whatever it is to him. Never!"

"Nonsense! You can learn to say anything if you try," declared Russ loftily.

"No," sighed Rose, who knew her limitations, "I can't. I can't even learn to say Con-stan-stan-stan-ple—You know!"

"Con-stan-ti-no-ple!" exclaimed Russ with emphasis.

"Yes. That's it," Rose said. "But, anyway, I can't say it."

"I'd like to know why not?" demanded her brother scornfully.

"'Cause I get lost in the middle of it," declared Rose, shaking her head. "It's too long, Russ."

"Well, 'Mr. John Scarbontiskil' is long," admitted Russ. "But if you practise from now, right on——"

"But what is the use of practising if we are not going there with daddy?"

"But maybe we'll go," said Russ hopefully.

"We have got to go to school. I don't mind," sighed Rose. "Only I do so love to travel about with daddy and mother."

"You can practise saying it on the chance of our going," her brother advised.

But Rose did not really think there was much use in doing that. She said so. She was not of so hopeful a disposition as Russ. He believed that "something would turn up" so that the six little Bunkers would be taken with daddy and mother to the far Southwest. Grandma Bell often spoke of a "silver lining" to every cloud, and Russ was hoping to see the silver lining to this cloud of Daddy Bunker's going away.

At any rate, the fact that Mr. Bunker had to go to Cowboy Jack's (we'll not call him Mr. Scarbontiskil, either, for it is too hard a name) was quite established that very afternoon. Daddy received another letter from his Pineville client, and he at once said to Mother Bunker:

"That settles it, Amy." Mrs. Bunker's name was Amy. "Golden is determined that nobody but me shall do the job for him. He offers such a good commission—plus transportation expenses—that I do not feel that I can refuse."

"Oh, Charles," said Mrs. Bunker, "I don't like to have you go so far away from us. It really is a great way to that town of Cavallo that you say is the nearest to Cowboy Jack's ranch."

"I'll take you all home to Pineville first. Then you will not be quite so far away from me," Daddy Bunker said reflectively.

So daddy and mother were no more happy at the prospect of his being separated from the family than were the children themselves. The six talked about the prospect of daddy's going a good deal. But, of course, they did not spend all their time bewailing this unexpected separation. Not at all! There was something happening to the six little Bunkers almost all the time, and this time was no exception.

The equinoctial storm seemed to have blown itself out by the next morning. As soon as the roads were dried up Daddy Bunker said they would have to leave Captain Ben and start back for Pineville. Meanwhile the children determined to have all the fun possible in the short time remaining to them at Grand View.

Bright and early on this morning appeared Tad Munson. Tad was the "runaway boy" in a previous story, and all those who have read "Six Little Bunkers at Captain Ben's" will remember him. He was a very likable boy, too, and Russ liked Tad particularly.

"They told me you Bunkers were going home soon, so I asked my father to let me come over once more to see you," Tad said, by way of greeting. "There's a lot of things you Bunkers haven't seen about here, I guess. I know you haven't seen Dripping Rock."

"What is Dripping Rock?" Vi promptly wanted to know. "What does it drip?"

"Not milk, anyway, or molasses," laughed Tad.

"It drips water, of course," Russ explained. "I have heard of it. You go up the road past the swamp. I know."

"That's right," said Tad. "It's not far."

"I want to go, too, to D'ipping Wock," Mun Bun declared.

"Of course you do," Rose told him. "And if mother lets us go——"

Mother did. As long as Tad was along and knew the way, she was sure nothing would happen to her little Bunkers. At least, nothing worse than usual. Something was always happening to them, she told daddy, whether they stayed at home or not.

"Don't go into the swamp, that is all," said Mother Bunker.

"Why not?" asked Vi.

"I know a riddle about a swamp," said Laddie eagerly. "Why is a swamp like what we eat for breakfast?"

"Goodness!" cried Rose. "That can't be. I had an egg and two slices of bacon for breakfast, and that couldn't be anything like a swamp."

"But you ate something else," cried Laddie delightedly. "You ate mush. And isn't a swamp just like mush?"

"Huh! You wouldn't think so if you ever tasted swamp mud," said Tad.

"But I guess that is a pretty good riddle after all," Russ told the little boy kindly. "For the mush and the swamp are both soft."

"And—and mushy," said Margy. "I think that's a very nice riddle, Laddie. Why do we eat swamps for breakfast?"

"Goodness! We don't!" exclaimed Rose. "Now, come along. If we are going to the Dripping Rock, we'd better start."

It was not far—not even in the opinion of Mun Bun. They took a road that led right back from the shore, and you really would not have known the sea was near at all when once you got into that path. For there were trees on both sides, and for half the way at least there were no open fields.

"I hear somebody calling," said Russ suddenly, as he led the way with Tad.

"Somebody shouting," said Tad. "I wonder what he wants!"

"I hear it," cried Rose suddenly. "Is he calling for help?"

"Hurry up," advised Tad. "I guess somebody wants something, and he wants it pretty bad."

"Well," said Russ, increasing his pace, but not so much so as to leave Mun Bun and Margy very far behind, "if he wants help, of course he wants it bad. Oh! There's the swamp."

They came to the opening. There were a few trees here on either side of the road, which was now made of logs laid down on the soft ground. Grass grew between the logs. There were pools of water, and other pools of very black mud with only tufts of tall grass growing between them.

"Oh!" cried Rose, who had very bright eyes, "I see him!"

"Who do you see?" demanded Tad, who was turning around and trying to look all ways at once.

"There! Can't you see him?" demanded Rose, with growing excitement. "Oh, the poor thing!"

Just then an unmistakable "bla-a-at!" startled the other children—even Tad Munson. He brought his gaze down from the trees into the branches of which he had been staring.

"Bla-a-at!" was the repeated cry, which at first the children had thought had been "Help!"

"And sure enough," Russ said confidently, "he is saying 'help!' just as near as he can say it."

"The poor thing!" sighed Rose again.

CHAPTER IV

WHAT WAS STUCK IN THE MUD

Russ began to whistle a tune, as he often did when he was puzzled. It was not that he was puzzled about the thing he saw—and which Rose had seen first—but at once Russ felt that he must discover a way to get the blatting object out of the mud.

"What do you know about that!" cried Tad Munson. "That's John Winsome's red calf. See! He's sunk clear to his backbone in the mud."

"Oh, dear me!" cried Rose. "The poor thing!"

She had said that twice before, but everybody was so excited that none of them noticed that Rose was repeating herself. In fact, both Vi and Margy said the very same thing, and in chorus:

"Oh, the poor thing!"

"Is that a red calf, Tad Munson?" asked Laddie. "For if it is, it's a riddle. Its head and its neck and its tail are all splattered with mud."

"It was a red calf when it went into the swamp, all right," said Tad with confidence. "I know that calf, all right. And John Winsome told me only this morning that he had lost it."

"Who put it in that horrid swamp?" Vi demanded.

"I guess it just wandered in," said Tad.

"And it is sinking down right now," Russ tried. "See it?"

Indeed the poor calf—a well grown animal—was in a very serious plight. It was eight or ten feet from the edge of the road where the logs were. And the calf had evidently struggled a good deal and was now quite exhausted. It turned its head to look at the children and blatted again.

"Oh, dear!" said Margy, almost in tears, "it is asking us to help it just as plain as it can."

"I'm going to run and tell John Winsome—right now I am!" shouted Tad, and he turned around and ran back along the road they had come just as fast as he could run.

But Russ stayed where he was. His lips were still puckered in a whistle and he was thinking hard.

"What can we do for the poor calf, Russ?" asked Rose.

She seemed to think that her brother would think up some way of helping the mired creature. No knowing how long Tad would be in finding the owner, and it looked as though the calf was sinking all the time.

Russ Bunker had quite an inventive mind. The other children were helpless in this emergency, but he began to see how he could help the calf stuck in the muddy swamp. He ran to the roadside fence, which was a good deal broken down just at the edge of the open swamp lands. The fence rails were so old and dry that Russ could pull them, one at a time, away from the posts. He dragged the first one to the spot where the calf was blatting so pitifully. Although these cedar rails had been split out of logs many years before, they were still very strong.

"Come on, Rose! You can help drag these rails too," cried Russ, quite excited by the thought that he might be able to save the calf before Tad Munson brought help.

"Oh! what are you going to do? Are you going to burn that poor calf like the Indians used to burn folks?" asked Vi, who remembered something she had heard at Uncle Fred's ranch. "You going to burn the calf at the stake?"

This was a horrifying thought, but even Laddie, who was very tender-hearted, was too much excited to think of this. He said to his twin sister:

"How silly, Vi! You couldn't burn those old rails on that wet place. The fire would go right out."

"Russ won't burn it, or let it drown either," Margy said, with much confidence in their older brother.

Meanwhile Russ and Rose were pulling off fence-rails and dragging them to the edge of the swamp. Then, while Rose brought more, Russ began to lay the rails on the quivering mire, side by side but about a foot apart, the ends of the first row of rails being only a few inches from the side of the calf.

Having made a foundation of four rails upon the soft muck, Russ began to lay the next tier across them, thus building a platform. It was a shaky platform, but he crept out upon it slowly and carefully and the lower rails did not sink much.

"Won't you sink down in the mud, too, if you do that, Russ?" asked Vi curiously. "Won't those old rails get splinters in your hands?"

"Oh!" cried Laddie, jumping up and down in his excitement, "then you'll be the riddle, Russ. 'I went out to the woodpile and got it'—you know."

"Maybe it's a riddle—what I'm going to do for the poor calf when I can reach him," their brother said. "I know I can get to him; but how can I pull him up out of the mud?"

This was a harder question to answer than one of Vi's. The rails did not sink much under Russ's weight, and he believed he could get within reach of the calf. But, having reached the animal, what could the boy do?

"Bla-a-at!" bawled the calf, his smutched head lifted out of the mire.

"Oh, dear! The poor bossy!" gasped Rose, staggering along with another rail. "How you going to help him, Russ?"

"Give me that rail," commanded her brother, standing up gingerly upon the crisscrossed rails. "I bet I can keep him from sinking any farther, anyway. And maybe Tad will find his owner before long."

Russ had just thought of something to do. He balanced himself carefully and took the last rail from Rose.

"Oh, Russ!" cried Vi, "your shoes are getting all muddy."

"Well, I can clean them, can't I?" panted the boy.

"How can you when you haven't any blacking and brush here?" asked Vi.

Russ paid her and her question no attention. He had too much to think of just then. He pointed the rail he held downward and pushed it into the mire just beyond the far end of the platform he had built. The calf bawled again, and struggled some more; but Russ knew he was not hurting the creature, although he could feel the end of the rail scraping down along the calf's side.

He pushed down with all his might until at least half the length of the rail was out of sight. It was poked down right behind the calf's forelegs. Russ thought that if he could pry up the fore-end of the calf, the animal could not drown in the mud.

This is what he tried to do, anyway. And although the calf began to struggle again, being evidently very much frightened, Russ was able to force the end of the rail up, and lifted the calf's head and shoulders.

"Oh, Russ, you're doing it!" cried Rose.

The other children jumped up and down in their delight, and praised him too. All but Mun Bun. He didn't say anything, for the very good reason that he was no longer there to say it!

Nobody had noticed the little boy for the last few minutes. Mun Bun always liked to help, and he had first followed Rose to try to pull a rail off the fence. This was too heavy for Mun Bun, so he had wandered along the road to find a rail or a stick or something that he could drag back to help make Russ Bunker's platform.

None of the others had noticed his absence, and Mun Bun was out of sight when Russ, with the help of Rose, bore down on the end of the fence rail far enough to hoist the calf half way out of the mire.

"Where's Mun Bun?" demanded Rose, looking around.

"Can you save the calf, Russ?" asked Vi.

Russ, however, like Rose, was instantly alarmed by the absence of Mun Bun. A dozen things might happen to the littlest Bunker here in the swamp.

"Where is he?" rejoined Russ. He jumped up and the rail began to tip again, dousing the poor calf into the mire.

"Don't, Russ!" screamed Rose. "He's going down again!"

Russ sat down on the fence rail, and the calf came up, bawling pitifully. It was a very serious problem to decide. If they ran to find Mun Bun, the calf would be lost. What could Russ Bunker do?

CHAPTER V

GOOD-BYE TO GRAND VIEW

"Didn't you—any of you—see which way he went?" Rose demanded of the other children. "Oh! if Mun Bun gets into the swamp——"

"Of course he won't," said Margy. "He isn't a bossy-calf."

"Of course he won't," added Laddie. "Mother told us not to, and Mun Bun will mind mother."

"Shout for him!" commanded Russ, and raised his own voice to the very top note in calling Mun Bun's name.

The chorus of calls brought no response from Mun Bun. Only an old crow cawed in reply, and of course he knew nothing about Mun Bun or where he had gone.

Russ got off the rail again in his excitement, and down went the calf!

"Oh, you mustn't!" gasped Rose. "You'll drown him."

"But I guess we've got to find Mun Bun," said Vi.

Russ, however, had another idea. He was frightened because of the little boy's disappearance, but he did not want to lose the calf, having already partly saved him from the mud.

"You and Laddie, Vi, come here and help Rose hold down the rail," said Russ.

"But I must go look for Mun Bun, too!" cried Rose.

"Wait a minute," said Russ, "and we'll all go and hunt for him."

Russ had noticed a post of the old fence that had rotted off close to the ground. It was quite a heavy post, but Russ was strong enough to drag it to the side of the miry pool where the calf was fixed. He rolled the post upon the platform, and then on the end of the rail which the other children were holding down.

The post did not stay there very firmly at first. It was not perfectly round and it was gnarled (which means lumpy), and it did not seem to want to stay in place at all. Russ, however, was very persevering. He was anxious too, to keep the poor calf from drowning in the mud. And at length he got the post fixed to suit him.

"Now get up," Russ told them, and Rose and Vi and Laddie stood up.

"That fixes it!" cried Laddie, in great excitement.

"It's all right if the calf doesn't struggle much while we are gone," said Russ doubtfully. "Which way did Mun Bun go?"

"He went on ahead, towards that Dripping Rock we started to see," said Vi. "I saw him start, but I didn't think he was going to run away."

So the five Bunkers started off hurriedly along the log road through the swamp, calling for Mun Bun as they went, and hoping he had not got into real trouble. And he had not come to any harm, although he had wandered some distance from the swampy pool where the calf was.

By and by Mun Bun heard them calling, and he called back. But he was so busy that he did not return. They ran on along the road and at last around a turn, and there was Mun Bun down on his hands and knees in the middle of the road, so much interested in what he was looking at that he did not at first give the others much of his attention.

"What are you doing, Mun Bun?" cried Rose, first to reach the little boy.

"Oh, what's that?" asked Vi, at once curious when she saw the object before Mun Bun.

"I dess it's a box," said Mun Bun, looking over his shoulder. "But sometimes it walks. I'm waiting to see it walk again."

"A walking box!" shouted Laddie. "I can make a riddle out of that, I know. When is a box not a box at all?"

"When it's a turtle!" exclaimed Russ, beginning to laugh.

"No, no!" said Laddie. "That isn't the answer. When it walks. That is the answer to my riddle, Russ."

"That is an awfully funny looking turtle," Rose said. "See how high up it is." None of them had ever seen a wood tortoise before, and the box-like, horny shell was not like that of the little mud-turtles in Rainbow River or the snapping turtle Laddie had found at Uncle Fred's.

The tortoise was so scared (for Mun Bun had been poking it with a stick) that its legs and head were drawn into the shell and it refused to move. Russ did not know but that the tortoise would bite, so he said they had all better go back to the calf. Mun Bun did not like to give up his new-found treasure, but he went back, clinging to Rose's hand and looking back at the tortoise as long as he could see it.

When they came to the place where the calf had been stuck in the mud there was Tad Munson and with him a man. The man had already dragged the calf out to the road and was wiping the mud off with a bunch of grass.

"I declare, you are smart young ones," said John Winsome. "I would not have lost this calf for a good deal. I thank you. I never would have got him out if you hadn't thought of those rails, sonny."

Russ did not much care about being called "sonny." He said that he might as well have been called "moony"—and he didn't go mooning about at all! Older folk were always calling him "young staver" and "chip of the old block," and things like that. They didn't mean any harm; but of course Russ, like other boys, did not fancy being called out of name. And "sonny" did not make the oldest Bunker feel dignified at all.

"Don't mind, Russ," said Rose in a soft little voice when the man had led the staggering calf away. "Don't mind if he did call you sonny. I guess he thinks you are pretty smart just the same. Anyway, we know you are."

"I would have helped you get the rails and build that platform if I had stayed," said Tad Munson. "But I don't know that I would ever have thought of using the rails to save that poor calf. You see, all I could think of was running for John Winsome."

"And I guess that was the first thing to think about," Russ observed, nodding. "Anyway, it's all over now and the calf is safe again. We might as well go on to the Dripping Rock and see what it looks like."

"Oh, yes!" cried Vi. "And find out what it drips."

They trooped along the road, and, coming to the place where Mun Bun had so earnestly studied the wood tortoise, the little Bunkers were surprised to find that the hard-shelled creature had totally disappeared.

"Oh!" mourned Mun Bun. "My turkle is gone. Somebody come and took him."

"No," Rose told the little boy. "He was watching you very slyly, and when he saw you had gone, he ran away just as fast as he could travel."

"He needn't have been so scared," said Mun Bun, in disgust. "I wouldn't have hurt him."

"But you were poking him with a stick, you know, and he prob'ly thought you might poke his eyes out. Come on; let's hurry to the Dripping Rock."

They did this, and Vi, in her curiosity, even got wetted a good deal with the water that dripped from the rock where the spring welled out of the ground and spattered over the lip of the stone basin on top of the big boulder. Ferns grew all about the pool of water below, and Rose and Vi and Margy gathered a lot of these to carry home to Mother Bunker.

"I want to pick ferns, I do!" cried Mun Bun. "I want to take mother the biggest bunch of all."

He worked so hard at pulling the ferns that he tired himself out. And that and the walk to the Dripping Rock and the excitement about the calf in the mud, added to the walk back to Captain Ben's bungalow, made Mun Bun very tired and not a little cross when he got home.

"I want to give these ferns to mother. And I want my face and hands washed. And I want bwead and milk and go to bed right away!" was Mun Bun's declaration.

Although it was only lunch time, they let him have his way, for Mun Bun often took a nap in the early afternoon and mother said it made him as bright as a new penny when he woke up again.

So it was the others, and not Mun Bun, who told their elders about the calf stuck in the mud.

The end of their stay at Captain Ben's bungalow had now come, and although all the little Bunkers were sorry to leave Captain Ben and remembered with delight all the fun they had had here at Grand View, home at Pineville beckoned them.

"Even if we have to go to school," said Russ, "it will seem like visiting at first. Don't you think so? Almost as though our vacation kept on—because we haven't been home much."

"Well," sighed Rose, to whom he spoke, "I sort of like to go to school. But if father goes 'way out West to that Cowboy Jack's, and without us," and she sighed again, "it will seem awfully hard, Russ."

"Maybe something will happen!" cried the oldest little Bunker suddenly.

But just what did happen, even Russ Bunker could not possibly have imagined.

CHAPTER VI

THE COAL STRIKE

Mother, of course, took Mun Bun and Margy back to Pineville by train. It was much too long a journey for them in an automobile. Mr. Bunker, with the four bigger little Bunkers (doesn't that sound funny?) drove in a motor-car and spent one night's sleep on the way at a very pleasant country inn.

They did not have quite so much excitement here as they had at the farmhouse on their way down to the shore. But Rose and Vi had a room all to themselves, and felt themselves quite grown-up travelers. Russ and Laddie were in a second bed in Mr. Bunker's room, and in the night Laddie must have had a very exciting dream because he began to kick about and thrash with his arms and woke up Russ very suddenly.

"Get off me!" cried Russ. "Stop!"

Then he became wide awake, sat up, and saw that it was not a dog jumping all over him, as he had supposed, but his brother.

"Why, Laddie!" he exclaimed, shaking the younger boy. "If you don't stop I'll have to get out and sleep on the floor."

"Oh!" gasped Laddie. "Am I sleeping?"

"Well, you're not now, I guess. But you were sleeping—and kicking, too."

"Oh!" said Laddie again. "I thought that old calf was pulling me down into the mud to take a bath. That—that must be a riddle, Russ."

"What's a riddle?" asked his brother, yawning.

"When is a dream not a dream?" asked Laddie promptly.

"I—ow!—don't know," yawned Russ.

"When you wake up," declared Laddie with conviction.

But Russ did not answer. He had snuggled down into his pillow and was asleep again.

"Well—anyway," muttered Laddie, "I guess that wasn't a very good riddle after all."

They got home to Pineville the next day, and as the automobile rolled into the Bunker yard mother and Norah, the cook, besides Mun Bun and Margy, were in the doorway. The two little folks at once ran screaming into the yard.

"There's a strike!" cried out Margy.

"You tan't go to school!" added Mun Bun.

"What do you mean—strike?" asked Russ wonderingly.

"That old thunder struck us. That's enough," said Rose, harking back to their exciting time in the old house at the seashore.

"Who got struck?" asked Violet. "Did it hurt them—like it did Mun Bun and me when the tree fell on us?"

"It's a coal strike," said Margy. "And the school can't have any coal."

Neither Rose nor Russ just understood this. What had a coal strike to do with their going to school?

But they found out all about it after a time. Something quite exciting had happened in Pineville while they had been down at Grand View. Of course, it happened in quite a number of other places at the same time; but only as the coal strike affected their home town did it matter at all to the six little Bunkers.

Daddy Bunker had plenty of coal in the cellar against the coming of cold weather when the furnace should be started. But everybody was not as fortunate—or as wise—as Daddy Bunker.

And in the school bins no coal had been placed early in the season. Suddenly the delivery of coal in cars to Pineville was stopped. The coal dealers in the town had no coal to deliver, although they had sold a great deal of it for delivery.

Frost had come. Indeed, the flowers and plants in the gardens were already blackened by the touch of Jack Frost's scepter. That meant that soon it would be so cold that little boys and girls could not sit in the big rooms of the schoolhouse unless there were warm fires to send the steam humming through the pipes and radiators.

"Here we are, three weeks late for school already, and no likelihood of coal coming into the town for another month. Of course there will be no school," Mother Bunker said decidedly. "I should not dare let the children go in any case unless the fires were built."

"Quite right," said Daddy Bunker. "And I presume the other people will feel the same about their children. School must be postponed again."

"Oh, bully!" cried Russ.

He shouted it out so loud that the older folks, as well as the children, looked at him in some amazement.

"What is bully?" asked Vi. "Do you mean a coal strike is bully? Why can't we have coal to burn? Who has got our coal?"

Nobody gave her questions much attention, which of course was not unusual. But Daddy Bunker began to laugh.

"I can see what is working in Russ's mind," he said. "You reason from the cause of a lack of coal, to an effect that you need not go to school?"

"I—I don't mind going to school," Rose said, a little doubtfully but looking at her elder brother.

"And I don't mind, either," said Russ promptly. "Only daddy is going to that Cowboy Jack's. And if we can't go to school for a month, why can't we go with daddy? We might as well."

"Oh! Oh!" cried the other children in chorus, seeing very plainly now what Russ had meant by saying the coal strike was "bully."

"Perhaps you are taking too much for granted," Mother Bunker said soberly. "Still, Charles, maybe I had better not unpack our trunks quite yet?"

"I'll see what the outlook is to-morrow morning," said Daddy Bunker quite soberly. "Anyway, I shall not start for the Southwest until day after to-morrow. Will that give you time, if——?"

"Oh, yes," said Mother Bunker, who had become by this time an expert in making quick preparations for leaving home. "Norah and Jerry will get on quite well here."

This was enough to set the six little Bunkers in a ferment. At least, to put their minds in a ferment. They were so excited and so much interested in the possibility of going away again that they could not "settle," as Norah said, to their ordinary pursuits.

Even Rose had by this time decided that she would be able perhaps to pronounce the name of the man Daddy Bunker was going to see—Mr. John Scarbontiskil.

"And, anyway," she told Russ, "maybe I won't have to talk to him much."

"You needn't mind that," said Russ kindly. "Daddy says everybody calls him Cowboy Jack. Daddy has met him and likes him, and he told me that Cowboy Jack likes children, although he has none of his own."

"Why hasn't he?" demanded Vi. "Don't they have little boys and girls down there on the ranch where he lives?"

"He hasn't got any," said Russ. "So he likes other people's children."

RUSS AND LADDIE GOT OUT THEIR COWBOY AND INDIAN SUITS. RUSS AND LADDIE GOT OUT THEIR COWBOY AND INDIAN SUITS.

Six Little Bunkers at Cowboy Jack's. (Page)

Russ and Laddie were very busy getting out their cowboy and Indian suits and having Norah mend them. Of course they would want to dress like other people did in the Southwest.

The coal strike in western Pennsylvania really did send the six little Bunkers off to the Southwest almost as soon as they had returned from the seashore and their visit to Captain Ben.

Daddy came home the next noon and said that coal enough to supply the Pineville school might not arrive before November. At least, there would be four full weeks before school could safely open.

"We might as well make a long holiday of it, Charles," said Mother Bunker, quite complacently.

For she, too, liked to travel, and had, by now, got used to journeying about with the children. Russ and Rose were so helpful, too, that a trip to Cavallo did not seem such a huge undertaking after all.

"Shall we take our bathing suits, Mother?" asked Rose.

"No bathing suits this time, for we are not going to the seashore," declared Mother Bunker.

But in repacking what few things had been unpacked there were two things forgotten. The children really did not have time to "count up" and see if they had all their most precious possessions with them.

It was after they were on the train the following morning, and Pineville station, with Norah and Jerry waving good-bye on the platform, was out of sight, that Rose suddenly discovered a lack that made her cry out in earnest.

"Oh! Oh! I've lost it!" she said.

"What you lost?" asked Vi.

"My watch!" gasped Rose.

"Oh, dear me! Your nice new wrist watch?" asked Mother Bunker admonishingly.

"Yes, ma'am," sighed Rose. "I—I haven't got it."

"Oh, my!" cried Laddie suddenly.

He was fumbling at his scarf and trying to look at it by pulling it out to its full length and squinting down his nose at its pretty pattern.

"And what's the matter with you, Laddie?" asked Daddy Bunker. "What have you lost?"

"Oh, my!" said Laddie, quite as dolefully as Rose had spoken. "I—I don't see my new stick-pin. It isn't here. I—I just guess I have lost it, too."

CHAPTER VII

THE SOUP JUGGLER

Rose was almost in tears when she found that her watch was lost. But although Laddie felt very bad about his missing stick-pin, he would not cry. Just the same, he did not feel as though he could make a riddle out of it.

"Now, Rose, and you, Laddie," said Mother Bunker admonishingly, as she seated them before her in one of the double seats of the Pullman car in which they had their reservations, "I want to know all about how you came to forget the watch and the pin—and just where you forgot them?"

Although Mother Bunker was usually very cheerful and patient with the children, this was a serious matter. Carelessness and inattention were faults that Mother Bunker was always trying to correct. For those two faults, as she pointed out so frequently, led often to much trouble, as in this case. The loss of the wrist watch and the stick-pin could not be passed over lightly.

Laddie shook his head very sorrowfully. "That is a riddle, Mother," he said. "I can forget things so easy that I forget how I forget them."

But Rose was thinking very hard, and she broke out with:

"Maybe I never had it there at all!"

"Where?" asked Mrs. Bunker, while the other children stood in the aisle or knelt on the seat behind to listen at the conference. "Where didn't you have it?"

"At home, Mother. I—I guess I haven't seen that watch since we were at Captain Ben's."

"Oh!" shouted Laddie. "That is just it! I left my stick-pin at the bungalow. I left it sticking in that cushion on the bureau in that room where Russ and Mun Bun and I slept. Of course I did."

"Are you sure, Laddie?" asked Mrs. Bunker. "I remember that I did not go into that room to see if anything was left. I should have done so, but we were in such a hurry."

"My rememberer is all right now," declared Laddie, with conviction. "That is where I left the pin."

"And you, Rose?" asked their mother.

"I—I don't know for sure," admitted Rose. "I can't remember where I had the watch last—or when I wore it last. But I do not believe I had it at all when we came home to Pineville."

"Well, Laddie is positive, and I suspect that you were quite as careless as he was," Mrs. Bunker said. "You should not be, Rose, for you are older."

"Oh, Mother! I am so sorry," cried Rose. "Don't you suppose we'll ever see my watch and Laddie's pin again?"

"We will write a letter to Captain Ben at once," said Mrs. Bunker, getting the writing pad and fountain pen out of her bag. "He has not left Grand View, and he may have already found them both. But, of course, we cannot be sure."

"He would know they belonged to Rose and Laddie, if he found them," said Russ, trying to comfort the others.

"Yes. If he cleans up the house he might find them. But it is likely that he will hire somebody to do that, and we cannot be sure that the person cleaning up is honest."

"Oh, how mean! To steal Rose's watch and Laddie's pin!" cried Russ.

"What makes them steal, Mother?" queried Vi.

"Because they have not been taught that other people's possessions are sacred," said Mrs. Bunker gravely. "You know, I tell all you children not to touch each other's toys or other things without permission."

"Well!" ejaculated Vi, "Laddie took my book."

"I didn't mean to keep it," cried her twin at once. "And, anyway, it wasn't a sacred book. It was just a story book."

"Stealing is an intention to defraud," explained their mother, smiling a little. "But Vi's book was just as sacred, or set apart, to her possession as anything could be."

"I—I thought sacred books were like the Bible and the hymn book," murmured Laddie wonderingly.

Which was of course quite so. It took Laddie some time, he being such a little boy, to understand that it was the fact of possession that was "sacred" rather than the article possessed.

However, Mother Bunker wrote the letter to Captain Ben, asking him to hunt all about the bungalow for both the wrist watch Rose had lost and the stick-pin Laddie was so confident now that he had left sticking in the cushion on the bureau in the bedroom. She also wrote a letter to Norah asking the cook to look for the lost articles.

"Now what will you do with them?" asked Vi, referring to the letters.

"Mail them," replied Mother Bunker.

"How will you mail them? Is there a post-box in the car?"

"No. But we will find a way of getting them into the mails," her mother assured the inquisitive Violet.

"I know!" cried Russ. "I saw the mailsack hanging on the hook at the railroad station down on the coast, and the train came along and grabbed it off with another hook."

"That is getting the mail on to the train," said Vi promptly. "But how do they get it off?"

When Mrs. Bunker had finished writing the letters and had sealed and addressed the envelopes she satisfied Vi's curiosity, as well as that of the other children, by giving the letters and a dime to the colored porter, who promised to mail them at the first station at which the train stopped.

Then they all trooped into the dining car for dinner, where daddy had already secured two tables for his party. They had a waiter all to themselves, and the children thought that he was a very funny man. In the first place, he was very black, and when he smiled (which was almost all the time) he displayed so many and such very white teeth that Mun Bun and Margy could scarcely eat their dinner properly, they looked so often at the waiter.

He was a colored man who liked children too. He said he did, and he laughed loudly when Vi asked him questions, although he couldn't answer all her questions any better than other people could.

"Why is he called a waiter?" Vi wanted to know. "For he doesn't wait at all. He is running back and forth to the kitchen at the end of the car all the time."

"That's a riddle," declared her twin soberly. "'When is a waiter not a waiter?'"

"You'll have to answer that one yourself, Laddie," said Daddy Bunker, laughing.

"When he's a runner," Laddie said promptly. "Isn't that a good riddle?"

"And he juggles dishes almost as good as that juggler we saw at the show," Russ declared.

"He must have almost as much skill as a juggler to serve his customers in this car," said Mrs. Bunker, watching the man coming down the aisle as the train sped around a sharp curve.

"Oh! Look there!" cried Rose, who was likewise facing the right way to see the waiter's approach.

The smiling black man was coming with a soup toureen balanced on one hand while he had other dishes on a tray balanced on his other hand. The car swayed so that the waiter began to stagger as though he were on the deck of a ship in a heavy sea.

"Oh! He's going!" sang out Russ.

The waiter jerked to one side, and almost dropped the soup toureen. Then he pitched the other way and his tray hit against one of the diners at another table.

"Look out what you're doing!" cried the man whom the tray had struck.

"Yes, sah! Yes, sah!" panted the waiter, and he tried to balance his tray.

But there was the soup toureen slipping from his other hand. He had either to drop the tray or the soup. Each needed the grasp of both his hands to secure it, and the waiter, losing his smile at last and uttering a frightened shout, made a last desperate attempt to retain both burdens.

"There he goes!" gasped Russ again.

"I guess he is a soup juggler," declared Laddie, staring with all his might. "He's got it!"

After all, the waiter showed wisdom in making his choice as long as a choice had to be made. Even Daddy Bunker, when he could stop laughing, voiced his approval. The tray and the viands on it flew every-which-way. But the waiter caught the hot soup toureen in both hands. It was so hot that he could only balance it first in one hand and then the other while the train finished rounding that curve.

"My head an' body!" gasped the poor waiter. "I done circulated de celery an' yo' watah glasses, suah 'nough. But I done save mos' of de soup," and he set the toureen down with a thump in front of Daddy Bunker.

The steward came running with a very angry countenance, and the people who had been spattered by the water sputtered a good deal. But Daddy Bunker, when he could recover from his laughter, interceded for the "soup juggler," and the incident was passed off as an accident.

When daddy paid his bill and tipped the very much subdued waiter, Laddie tugged at his father's sleeve and whispered:

"What is it, Son?" asked Mr. Bunker, stooping down to hear what the little boy whispered.

"Ask him if he will juggle the soup again if we come in here to eat?"

But Mr. Bunker only laughed and herded his flock back into the other car. The children, however, thought the incident very funny indeed, and they hoped to see the juggling waiter again when they ate their next meal in the dining car.

Mother Bunker had brought a nicely packed basket for supper (Nora O'Grady had made the sandwiches and the cookies) and she sent daddy into the buffet car for milk and tea.

"The children get just as hungry on the train as they do when they are playing all day long out-of-doors," she told daddy. "But they must not eat too much while we are traveling. And I have to shoo the candy boy away every half hour."

The boy who sold magazines and candy interested Russ and Laddie very much. Russ thought that he might become a "candy butcher" when he grew up, although at first he had decided to be a locomotive engineer.

"It must be lots nicer to sell candy than to work an engine," Laddie said. "You get your hands all oil in an engine."

"Where does the oil come from?" asked Vi, who had not asked a question since she had seen the waiter "juggle" the soup toureen. "What does an engine have oil for? Do they keep it in a cruet, like that cruet on the table in the hotel we stopped at coming up from Grand View?"

And perhaps she asked even more questions, but these are all we have time to repeat right now. For evening had come, and soon the little Bunkers would be put to bed. Although they had two sections of the sleeping car, there was none too much room when the porter let down the berths and hung the curtains for them.

Besides, even after the little folks had all got quiet, peace did not reign for long in that sleeping car. The very strangest thing happened. Even Russ couldn't have invented it.

But I will have to tell you about it in the next chapter.

CHAPTER VIII

AN ALARM AND A HOLD-UP

Of course, the six little Bunkers were just ordinary children, although they sometimes had extraordinary adventures. And confinement for only a few hours in a Pullman car had made them very restless. It was impossible for them always to keep quiet, and their running up and down the aisles, and their exclamations about what they saw, sometimes annoyed other passengers just a little.

Most of the passengers in this car were people, fortunately, who liked children and could appreciate how difficult it was for the six to be always on their best behavior. And the passengers could not but admire the way in which Daddy and Mother Bunker controlled the exuberance of the six.

But there was one man who had scowled at the little Bunkers almost from the very moment they had boarded the train at Pineville. That man seemed to say to himself:

"Oh, dear! here is a crowd of children and they are going to annoy me dreadfully."

And, of course, as he expected to be annoyed, there was scarcely anything the Bunkers did or said but what did annoy him. He was a very fat man, and the car was sometimes too warm for him, and he was always complaining to the porter about something or other, and altogether he was a very miserable man indeed on that particular journey.

Maybe he was a nice man at home. But it is doubtful if he had any children of his own, and probably nobody's children would have suited him at all! Mun Bun and Margy made friends with almost everybody in the car but the fat man. He would not even look at Mun Bun when the little fellow staggered along the car, from seat to seat, and looked smilingly up into the fat man's red face.

"Go away!" said the fat man to Mun Bun.

Mun Bun's eyes grew round with wonder at the man's cross speech. He could not understand it at all. He looked at the fat man in a very puzzled way, and then went back to Mother Bunker's seat.

"Muvver," he said soberly, "do you got pep'mint?"

"I think you have eaten all the candy that is good for you now, Mun Bun," said Mother Bunker.

"No," said Mun Bun earnestly. "Not tandy. Pep'mint for ache," and he rubbed himself about midway of his body very suggestively.

"Mun Bun! are you ill?" demanded his mother anxiously. "Are you in pain, you poor baby?"

He explained then that he did not need the "pep'mint"; but knowing that Mother Bunker sometimes gave it to him when he had pain, he said he thought the man up the aisle would like some for the same reason.

"Better ask him," suggested Daddy Bunker, who had noted the unhappy face of the fat man.

Mun Bun did this. He asked the man very politely if he needed "pep'mint." But all the cross passenger said was:

"Go on away! You are a nuisance!"

So Mun Bun went back to daddy and mother in rather a subdued way, for he was not used to being treated so. Mun Bun liked to make friends wherever he went.

Perhaps the fat man was the only person in the car who was glad when the Bunker children went to bed. He went into the smoking room while his own berth was being made up, and when he came back to the berths, daddy and mother, as well as most of the other passengers, had retired. The car was soon after that pretty quiet.

Russ and Laddie were in the upper berth over daddy and Mun Bun. The boys in the upper berth had been asleep for some little time when Russ woke up—oh, quite wide awake!

There was something going on that he could not understand. Whether this mysterious something had awakened him or not, Russ lay straining his ears to catch a repetition of the sound. Then it came—a sound that made the boy "creep" all over it was so shuddery!

"Laddie! Laddie!" he whispered, nudging the boy next to him. "Don't you hear it?"

Laddie was not easily awakened. When Laddie went to sleep it was, as the children say, "for keeps." Russ had to punch him with his elbow more than once before the smaller boy awakened.

"Oh, oh! Is it morning?" murmured Laddie.

"Listen!" hissed Russ right in his ear. "That man's being mur—murdered!"

"Mur—murdered?" quavered Laddie in response. "You—you tell daddy about it, Russ Bunker. Don't you tell me. I don't believe he is, anyway. Who's mur—murderin' him?"

"I don't know who's doing it," admitted Russ, shaking as much as Laddie was.

"How do you know it's—it's being done?" repeated Laddie, his doubt growing as he became more fully awake.

"He says so. He says so himself. And if he says he's being murdered, he ought to know—Oh!"

Again the doleful sound reached their ears, this time Laddie hearing as well as Russ the moaning of a voice which uttered a muffled cry of "Mur-r-rder!"

"There! What did I tell you?" gasped Russ. "I'm—I'm going to tell daddy."

"Wait for me! Wait, Russ Bunker! I'm going with you," Laddie cried. "I don't want to stay here and be mur—murdered, too!"

That was an awful word, anyway. Russ crept over the edge of the berth at the foot and dropped down behind the curtain. Laddie was right behind him, and in fact came down first upon Russ's shoulders and then slipped to the floor of the car.

Before they could get inside daddy's curtain—a place which spelled safety to their disturbed imaginations—they heard the moaning voice again groan:

"Mur-r-rder!"

It was an awful choking cry—just like a hen squawked when Jerry Simms grabbed it by the neck and had his hand on the hen's windpipe!

"He's mur—murderin' him all right," chattered Laddie, tugging at Russ's pajama jacket. "Are—are you going to stop it, Russ?"

Russ had no idea of going himself to the rescue of the victim; he had only thought of waking daddy. But now he put his head outside the curtain and looked into the narrow aisle of the sleeping car. The first thing he saw was the colored porter, his cap on awry, his eyes rolling so that their whites were very prominent, stalking up the aisle in a crouching attitude with the little stool he sometimes sat on in the vestibule gripped by one leg as a weapon.

"It's the porter!" whispered Russ huskily.

"Is—is he being mur—murdered?" stuttered Laddie.

"He—he looks more as though he was going to do the mur-murdering," confessed Russ.

Laddie would not look; but Russ could not take his eyes off the approaching porter. The colored man crept nearer, nearer—and then suddenly he snatched away the curtain almost directly across the aisle from where the two little Bunkers stood.

There was nobody in that lower berth but the fat man before mentioned! He lay on his back with his knees up, his face very red, his eyes tightly closed. Again there issued from his lips the stifled cry of "Mur-r-rder!"

"Fo' de lan's sake!" exclaimed the porter, dropping his stool and grabbing the fat passenger by the shoulder. "I suah 'nough thunk somebody was bein' choked to deaf. Wake up, Mistah White Man! Ain't nobody a-murderin' of yo' but yo'self."

The fat man's eyes opened wide at that and he glared around. He saw the face of the porter at last and blinked his eyes for a moment. Then he sighed.

"I—I guess I was asleep. Must have been dreaming," he stammered gruffly.

"Say, Mistah!" the porter replied, "if yo' sleep like dat always, you bettah have a car by yo'self. For yo' ain't goin' to let nobody else sleep in peace. Turn over! Yo's on your back."

Russ and Laddie could only stare, and some of the other passengers began to open their curtains and ask questions of the porter. The fat man grabbed his own curtain away from the colored man and quickly shut himself in again.

"All right! All right!" said the porter, picking up his stool and going back to his place. "Ain't nobody killed yet. Guess we goin' to have peace now fo' a while."

Daddy Bunker awoke too and sent his little folks back to bed, and Russ and Laddie did not wake up again till broad daylight. They had to tell the other little Bunkers before breakfast about what had happened; but they never saw the fat man again, for he left the train at a station quite early.

There were other things to interest the little Bunkers. In the first place, it began to rain soon after they got up. A rainy day at home was no great cross for the children to bear. There was always the attic to play in. But on the train, with the rain beating against the windows and not much to see as the train hurried on, the children began to grow restless.

It was reported that the heavy rains ahead of them had done some damage to the railroad, and the speed of the train was reduced until, by the middle of the forenoon, it seemed only to creep along. The conductor, who came through the car once in a while, told them that there were "washouts" on the road.

"What's washouts?" demanded Vi. "Is it clothes on clotheslines, like Norah's washlines? Why don't they take the wash in when it rains so?"

She really had to be told what "washout" meant, or she would have given daddy and mother no peace at all. And the other children were interested in the possibility that the train might be halted by a big hole in the ground where the tracks ought to be.

Every time the train slowed down they were eagerly on tiptoe to see if the "washout" had come. They were finally steaming through a deep cut in the wooded hills when, of a sudden, the brakes were applied and the train came to a stop with such a shock that the little Bunkers were all tumbled together—although none of them was hurt.

"Here's the washout! Here's the washout!" cried Laddie eagerly.

"Can we go look out of the door, Mother?" asked Rose.

For some of the passengers were standing in the vestibule and the door was open. Daddy got up and went with the children, all clamorous to see the hole in the ground that had halted the train.

But it was not a hole at all. It was something so different from a hole, or a washout as the children had imagined that to be, that when they saw it they were very much excited and surprised.

CHAPTER IX

THE BIG ROCK THAT FELL DOWN

"Where is it? Let me see it!" was Vi's cry, as she rushed out into the vestibule ahead of Daddy Bunker and her brothers and sisters.

Vi was so curious that she thought she just had to be first. Daddy Bunker tried to restrain her, for he was afraid she would fall down the car steps and out upon the cinder path beside the rails. And although it had now ceased raining, she might easily have been hurt, if not made thoroughly wet.

"Oh, Vi's going to see the washout first!" cried Laddie, who did not like to play second when his twin wanted to be first.

"Now, wait!" commanded daddy. "You shall all see what there is to see——"

"I want to see the wash up on the clotheslines," said Mun Bun, breaking into his father's speech.

"Well, if you will be patient," Mr. Bunker said, smiling, "I think we'll all have a fair view of the wonder. But the 'washup' isn't going to be just what you think it is, Mun Bun."

Nor was it just what any of the six little Bunkers thought it would be—as I said before. Daddy went down the steps first and then turned and "hopped" the children down to the cinder path, one after the other. Only Russ, who came last, jumped down without any assistance.

It was still very wet and all about were shallow puddles. But the rain itself had ceased. In places, especially in the ditches alongside the railroad bed, the water had torn its way through the earth, leaving it red and raw. And big stones had been unearthed in the banks of the ditches and in some cases carried some distance away from where they had formerly lain.

"Why, that isn't a hole in the ground at all!" cried Laddie, first to realize that what had made the train stop was something different from what they had all expected.

"Oh!" shouted Violet. "It's a great, big rock that's fallen down the hill."

"Well," said Russ, soberly, "I guess it's a washout at that. For the rain must have washed it out of the hillside. See! There is the hole up there in the bank."

"You are right, Russ," said Daddy Bunker. "It is a washout, and it will take a long time to get that big rock off of the track so that the train can go on."

The rock that had fallen completely blocked the west-bound track, as daddy said. And a good deal of earth and gravel had fallen with it so that the rails of the east-bound track were likewise buried. There was already a gang of trackmen clearing away this gravel; but, as the children's father had told them, it would take many hours to remove the great boulder.

"Suppose our train had been going by when the rock fell?" suggested Russ to Rose.

"What would the rock have done to us?" asked Vi, who heard her brother say this.

"I guess it would have done something," replied Russ solemnly.

"It would have pushed us right off the track," declared Rose, nodding her head.

"And what would it have done then?" demanded Vi.

"I wish you wouldn't, Vi," complained her twin suddenly.

"Wish I wouldn't what?"

"Ask so many questions."

"Why not?"

"Why, I was just thinking of a riddle about that big rock; and now it's all gone," sighed Laddie.

"No, it isn't gone at all," Vi said wonderingly. "Daddy says it will take hours to move it."

"Oh! That old rock!" said Laddie. "I meant my riddle. That's all gone."

"I guess it wasn't a very good riddle, then, if it went so easy," said the critical Vi. "Oh, look there!"

"At what?" exclaimed her twin, following Vi to the fence beside the railroad bed.

"See that path, Laddie? I guess we could climb right up that hill and see down into that hole where the big rock washed out."

"So we could," agreed the boy. "Let's."

Daddy and the other children were some yards away, but in plain sight. Indeed, they would be in sight if Vi and Laddie climbed to the very top of the bank. It did not seem to either of the twins that they needed to ask permission to climb the path when daddy was so near and could see them by just looking up. So they hopped over the low fence and began to climb.

It was an easy path, almost all of stone, and the rain had washed it clean. It was great fun to be so high above the railroad and look down upon the crowd of passengers from the stalled train and upon the workmen. The two explorers could see into the hole washed in the hillside, and it was much deeper than it had looked to be when they stood below. There was a puddle of muddy water in it, too.

"Guess we don't want to fall into that," said Laddie, and Vi did not even ask why not. "Let's go on to the top. We can see farther."

Vi was quite willing to go as far as her twin did. And there really seemed to be no reason why they should not go. It would be hours before that rock could be moved, and of course the train could not go on until that was done.

They reached the top of the bank. Here was a great pasture which sloped away to a piece of woods. Although the ground was wet, it had stopped raining some time before and a strong wind was blowing. This wind had dried the grass and weeds and the twins did not wet their feet. And——

"Oh!" squealed Vi, starting away from the edge of the bank on a run. "See the flowers! Oh, see the flowers, Laddie!"

Laddie saw the flowers quite as soon as she did, but he did not shout about it. He followed his sister, however, with much promptness, and both of them began to pick the flowering weeds that dotted the pasture.

"We'll get a big bunch for mother. Won't she be glad?" went on Vi.

Mother Bunker was supposed to have a broad taste in flowers, and every blossom the children found was brought for her approval. In a minute the twins were so busy gathering the blossoms of wild carrots and other weeds that they forgot the train, and the big rock that had fallen, and even the fact that they had climbed the bank without permission.

At length Laddie stood up to look abroad over the great field. Perhaps he had pulled the blossoms faster than Vi. At any rate, he had already a big handful. Suddenly he caught sight of something that interested him much more than the flowers did.

There was a stone fence near by which divided the fields. And on the fence something flashed into view and ran along a few yards—something that interested the boy immensely.

"Oh, look, Vi!" cried Laddie. "There's a chippy!"

"What chippy? Who's chippy?" demanded Vi excitedly.

"There he goes!" shouted Laddie. "A chipmunk!"

He dropped his bunch of blossoms and started for the stone fence. Vi caught a glimpse of the whisking chipmunk, and she dropped her flowers and ran after her brother.

"Oh, let me catch him! Let me catch him!"

The chipmunk ran along the stone fence a little way, and then looked back at the excited children. He did not seem much frightened. Perhaps he had been chased by children before and knew that he was more than their match in running.

At any rate, that chipmunk drew Laddie and Vi on to the very edge of the woods, and then, with a flirt of its tail, it disappeared into a hole and they could not find him.

Laddie and Vi were breathless by that time, and they had to sit down and rest. They looked back over the field. It was a long way to the brink of the bank from which they could see the train and the passengers.

"I—I guess we'd better go back," said Laddie.

"And mother's flowers!" exclaimed Vi. "Do you know where you dropped them?"

"I dropped mine just where you dropped yours, I guess," returned her brother.

"We'll go pick them up. Come on."

They were both tired when they started to trudge back up the hill. And just as they started they heard a long blast of a whistle, and then two short blasts.

"What do you suppose that is?" asked Vi.

"It's the engine. Oh, Vi! maybe it's going to start without us," and Laddie began to run, tired as he was.

"Wait for me, Laddie! It can't go—you know it can't. The big rock is in the way."

But they were both rather frightened, and they did not stop to find their flowers. The possibility that the train might go off and leave them filled the two children with alarm. They ran on as hard as they could, and Vi fell down and soiled her hands and her dress.

She was beginning to cry a little when Laddie came back for her and took her hand. He was frightened, too; but he would not show it by crying—not then, anyway.

"Come on, Vi," he urged. "If that old train goes on with daddy and mother and the rest, I don't know what we shall do!"

CHAPTER X

WHERE ARE THE TWINS?

The wrecking crew with their big derrick and other tools had not yet arrived in the cut where the stalled west-bound train, on which rode the Bunker family, had stopped. But the section gang had shoveled away the dirt and gravel from the east-bound track.

Russ and Rose and Margy and Mun Bun had found plenty to interest them in watching the shovelers and in listening to the men passengers talking with daddy and some of the train crew. Finally Mun Bun expressed a desire to go back into the car, and Rose went with him. As they were climbing the steps into the vestibule a brakeman came running forward along the cinder path beside the tracks.

"All aboard! Back into the cars, people!" he shouted. "We're going to steam back. Get aboard!"

Russ and Margy being the only Bunker children in sight, Mr. Bunker "shooed" them back to the Pullman car. He saw Rose and Mun Bun disappearing up the high steps, and he presumed Laddie and Violet were ahead. The train had started and the four children and daddy came to mother's seat before it was discovered that there were two little Bunkers missing.

"Oh, Charles!" gasped Mrs. Bunker. "Where are they?" The train began to move more rapidly. "They are left behind!"

"No, Amy, I don't think so," Mr. Bunker told her soothingly. "I looked all about before I got aboard and there wasn't a chick nor child in sight. I was one of the last passengers to get aboard. The section men had even got upon their handcar and were pumping away up the east-bound track. There is not a soul left at that place."

"Then where are they?" cried Mother Bunker, without being relieved in the least by his statement.

"I think they are aboard the train—somewhere. They got into the wrong car by mistake. We will look for them," said Mr. Bunker.

So he went forward, while Russ started back through the rear cars, both looking and asking for the twins. As we quite well know, Vi and Laddie were not aboard the train at all, and the others found this to be a fact within a very few minutes. Back daddy and Russ came to the rest of the family.

"I knew they were left behind!" Mother Bunker declared again, and this time nobody tried to reassure her.

Her alarm was shared by daddy and the older children. Even Margy began to cry a little, although, ordinarily, she wasn't much of a cry-baby. She wanted to know if they had to go on to Cowboy Jack's and leave Vi and Laddie behind them—and if they would never find them again.

"Of course we'll find them," Rose assured the little girl. "They aren't really lost. They just missed the train."

Daddy hurried to find their conductor and talk with him. He came back with the news that the train was only going to run back a few miles to where there was a cross-over switch, and then the train would steam back again into the cut on the east-bound track. The conductor promised to stop there so Mr. Bunker could look for the lost children.

But Mother Bunker was much alarmed, and the children kept very quiet and talked in whispers. Although Russ and Rose spoke cheerfully about it to the other children, they were old enough to know that something really dreadful might have happened to the twins.

"I guess nobody could have run off with them," whispered Russ to his sister.

"Oh, no! There were no Gypsies or tramps anywhere about. Anyway, we didn't see any."

"They weren't carried off. They walked off," said Russ decidedly. "Maybe they will be back again waiting for the train."

They all hoped this would be the fact. The train finally stopped and then steamed ahead again and ran on to the east-bound track that had been cleared of all other traffic so that the passenger train could get around the landslide. Mr. Bunker and Russ went out into the vestibule so as to jump off the train the moment it stopped in the cut. The conductor and one of the brakemen got off too, but other passengers were warned to remain aboard. The train could not halt here for long.

Russ ran around the big rock that had fallen on the other track, and up the road a way. But there was no sign of Vi and Laddie. Mr. Bunker saw the path up the bank, and he climbed just as the twins had and reached the top.

The big pasture was then revealed to the anxious father; but Vi and Laddie were nowhere in view. Why! Daddy Bunker didn't even see the chipmunk

Laddie and his sister had chased. Daddy Bunker shouted and shouted. If the twins had been within sound of his voice they surely would have answered. But no answer came.

"You'll have to come down from there, Mr. Bunker!" called the conductor of the train. "We can't wait any longer. We're holding up traffic as it is."

So Mr. Bunker came down to the railroad bed, very much worried and hating dreadfully to go back and tell Mother Bunker and the rest of the little Bunkers that the twins were not to be found.

There was nothing else to be done. Where the twins could have disappeared to was a mystery. And just what he should do to trace Vi and Laddie their father could not at that moment imagine.

The train started again, but ran slowly. Mrs. Bunker did not weep as Margy did, and as Rose herself was inclined to do. But she was very pale and she looked at her husband anxiously.

"My poor babies!" she said. "I think we will all have to get off the train at the next station, Charles, and wait until Vi and Laddie are found."

Daddy Bunker could not say "no" to this, for he did not see any better plan. Of course they could not go on to Cowboy Jack's ranch and leave Vi and Laddie behind.

The other passengers in the car took much interest in the Bunkers' trouble. Most of the men and women had grown fond of Violet, in spite of her inquisitiveness, and all admired Laddie Bunker. It seemed a really terrible thing that the two should have become separated from their parents and the other children.

"Something is always happening to us Bunkers," confessed Russ. "But what happens isn't often as bad as this. I don't see what Vi and Laddie could have been thinking of."

We know, however, that the twins had been thinking of nothing but gathering flowers and chasing a chipmunk until that train whistle had sounded. How the twins did run then across the pasture and up to the very verge of the high bank overlooking the railroad cut!

"Oh, the train's gone!" shrieked Vi, when she first looked down.

"And the workmen are gone too," gasped Laddie.

There was nobody left in the cut, and both the train and the handcar on which the section hands had traveled, were out of sight. It was the loneliest place that the twins had ever seen!

"Now, see what we've done," complained Vi, between her sobs. "We ran away and lost mother and daddy and the others. They've gone on to Cowboy Jack's and left us here."

"Then we didn't run away from them," Laddie said more sturdily. "They ran away from us."

"That doesn't make any difference," complained his sister. "We—we're lost and can't be found."

"Say!" cried Laddie suddenly, "how do you s'pose that train hopped over that rock?"

This point interested Vi at once. It was a most astonishing thing. If the train had gone on to Cowboy Jack's, it surely had got over that big rock in a most wonderful way.

"How did it get over the rock?" Vi began. "Did it fly over? I never saw the wings on that engine, did you? And if the engine did fly over, it couldn't have dragged the cars with it, could it?"

"Oh, don't, Vi!" begged Laddie, much puzzled. "I couldn't tell you all that. Maybe they had some way of lifting the train around the rock. Anyway, it's gone."

"And—and—and what shall we do?" began Vi, almost ready to cry again.

"We have just got to follow on behind it. I guess daddy will miss us and get off and come back to look for us after a while."

"Do you suppose he will?"

"Yes," said Laddie with more confidence, as he thought of his kind and thoughtful father. "I am sure he will, Vi. Daddy wouldn't leave us alone on the railroad with no place to go and nothing to eat."

At this Vi was reminded that they had not eaten since breakfast, and although it was not yet noon, she declared that she was starving!

"You can't be starving yet," Laddie told her, with scorn. "We haven't been lost from the train long enough for you to be starving, Violet Bunker."

"Well, Laddie, I just know we will starve here if the train doesn't come back for us."

"Maybe another train will come along and we can buy something from the candy boy. You 'member the candy boy on our train? I've got ten cents in my pocket."

"Oh, have you? That will buy four lollipops—two for you and two for me. I guess I wouldn't starve so soon if I had two lollipops," admitted Vi.

"I guess you won't starve," Laddie told her without much sympathy. "Now we must climb down to the tracks and start after daddy's train."

"Do you suppose we can catch it? Will it stop and wait when daddy finds out we're not on it? And are you sure he'll come back looking for us? Shall we get supper, do you s'pose, Laddie, just as soon as we get on the train? For I'm awfully hungry!"

Her twin could not answer. Like the other Bunkers, he was nonplussed by some of Vi's questions. Nor did he have much idea of how Daddy Bunker was going to stop the train, which he supposed had gone ahead, and return to meet Vi and him trudging along the railroad tracks.

CHAPTER XI

THE MAN WITH THE EARRINGS

The twins got out of the cut between the two hills after a time, and then it was long past noon and Laddie was hungry as well as Vi. It seemed terrible to the Bunker twins to have money to spend and no way to spend it. They might just as well have been on a desert island, like that man Robinson Crusoe about whom Rose read to them.

"I know a riddle about that Robinson Crusoe man. Yes, I do!" suddenly exclaimed Laddie.

"What is the riddle, Laddie? Do I know it?"

"You can try to guess it, Vi," said the eager little boy. "Now listen! 'How do we know Robinson Crusoe had plenty of fish to eat?'"

"'Cause the island was in the water," said Vi promptly. "Of course there were fish."

"Well, that isn't the answer," Laddie said slowly.

"Why isn't it?"

"Because—because the answer is something about Friday. You fry fish, you know—And anyway, Crusoe's man was named Friday."

"Pooh!" scoffed Vi. "You fry bacon and eggs and lots of other things, besides those nice pancakes Norah makes for breakfast when we're at home. I don't think much of that riddle, Laddie Bunker, so now!"

"I guess it is a good riddle if I only knew how to ask it," complained her twin. "But somehow I've got it mixed up."

"Don't ask any more riddles like that. They make me hungry," declared Vi. "And there isn't a candy shop or anything around here."

She came very near to speaking the exact truth that time. On both sides of the railroad track where they now walked so wearily there seemed to be almost a desert. There were neither houses nor trees, and although the country was rolling, it was not at all pleasant in appearance.

And how tired their feet did become! If you have ever walked the railroad tracks (which you certainly must never do unless grown people are with you, for it is a dangerous practise) you know that stepping from tie to tie between the rails is a very uncomfortable way to travel, because the ties are not laid at equal distances apart. First Vi and Laddie had to take a short step and then a long step. And if they missed the tie in stepping, their shoes crunched right down into the wet cinders, for the ground by no means was all dried up since the heavy rain.

"Oh, me, I'm so tired!" complained Vi, after a while.

"So'm I," confessed her twin brother.

"And I don't see daddy coming for us," added Vi, her voice tremulous with tears again.

"I SEE SOMETHING!" CRIED LADDIE. "I SEE SOMETHING!" CRIED LADDIE.

Six Little Bunkers at Cowboy Jack's. (Page)

"I see something!" cried Laddie suddenly and hopefully. He did not want his sister to begin crying.

"Is it Daddy Bunker?" demanded Vi, looking ahead eagerly.

"It's a house—right beside the railroad," said Laddie, quickening his own pace a little and trying to drag Vi along, as he still held her hand.

"Where? Where is the house?" demanded Vi anxiously. "I don't see any house."

"Well, it's a very small house. But there it is," said her brother, pointing ahead with confidence.

"Oh! I see it, Laddie," cried Vi. "Oh, what a little house it is—and so close to the tracks! Do you suppose anybody lives in that little house?"

"I don't know. It is small," admitted Laddie.

"Maybe a dog lives in it. It isn't much bigger than Mr. Striver's dog-house at home in Pineville."

"I guess it isn't a dog-house. Anyway, we'll see."

"Maybe it's a candy store," suggested the reviving Vi more cheerfully. "If you could spend your dime, Laddie, for something to eat, I'd feel a whole lot better, I guess."

"Oh, I know what it is, Vi!" exclaimed the boy suddenly. "It's a riddle."

"There you go again with your old riddles," sniffed Vi. "We can't eat riddles."

"This is a good one," declared her brother cheerfully. "I'm going to ask you: What looks like a dog-house, but isn't a dog-house?"

"I don't know. A hen-house, Laddie?"

"Pooh! They don't build hen-houses right down beside railroad tracks, and just where a road crosses the tracks."

"Don't they? What do they build there, then?"

"Why," cried Laddie, quite delighted at his discovery, "a flagman's house. That is what that little house is, Vi. A flagman stays there to stop people from crossing the tracks when the train is coming. There! There's the flagman now. See him?"

Just as Laddie spoke so excitedly a man came out of the little house, and he bore a flag in his hand. Unnoticed by the children, there had begun behind them a rumbling sound, and the rails between which they walked began to hum. There was a train coming from the east.

The flagman unrolled his flag, and then he looked both ways along the road that crossed the railroad. Then he turned and saw the two little folks coming toward him. At sight of them he became much more excited than the children were.

"Look out-a da train!" he shouted. "Look out-a da train!"

"What does he say?" asked Vi curiously.

The flagman began to wave his arms and the flag, and ran toward the twins. He was a man with a very dark face, and his hair was black and curly. But what interested Laddie and Vi most about the flagman was that he wore big gold rings in his ears.

"Look out-a da train!" shouted the flagman again.

"I never saw a man wearing earrings before," said Vi soberly. "And he acts awfully funny, doesn't he?"

The little girl began to feel a bit afraid of the strange man. She stopped walking ahead and pulled back on her brother's hand.

"I guess he doesn't mean any harm," said Laddie doubtfully.

But drawn away by Vi, he stepped with her off the ties into the path between the east-and west-bound tracks. The flagman stopped running, but still gestured to the children. And just then, quite startling in the twins' ears, sounded the long drawn shriek of a locomotive whistle.

Laddie and Vi glanced behind them. Around the curve, out of the railroad cut in which their adventure had begun, was coming a big locomotive drawing a long passenger train. The man with the earrings reached Vi and Laddie the very next moment.

"Look-a da train!" he cried. "You bambinoes want-a get run over—yes?"

"We're not Bambinoes, Mister," said Laddie. "We're Bunkers."

Vi could not quench her usual curiosity, although the man seemed so strange in her eyes. She asked:

"Why do you wear rings in your ears? Please, why do you wear 'em?"

CHAPTER XII

CAVALLO AT LAST

The man with the earrings led the twins over the other track so that they would be sufficiently far from the train. To his surprise the engine began to slow down, the engineer and fireman waved their hands as they leaned out of the window and door of the cab, and by and by the train rumbled to a stop.

"That looks just like our train," Laddie announced confidently. "Only ours was traveling on this nearer track. Maybe the two trains were racing and our train got ahead in spite of the washout."

Vi stuck to her subject. She scarcely looked at the train when it first stopped. Her gaze was fastened upon the flagman who had showed such anxiety for her safety and that of Laddie.

"Say, please, Mister," she continued to ask, "what makes you wear earrings?"

A Pullman coach had halted just opposite the spot where the twins and the flagman stood. They saw several people at two of the windows, waving to them. Then Russ Bunker popped out of the front door of the car and down the steps.

"Look! Look! Here they are!" Russ shouted, as he ran toward his brother and sister and the man who wore earrings.

"Why, Russ Bunker!" ejaculated Vi, "how did you come on that train? Were you left behind, too?"

"Come on! Hurry up!" the oldest Bunker boy replied. "This is our train. And the engineer will stop only a minute. Do you know, it costs three dollars and thirty-three and a third cents every time the train stops? The brakeman told me so."

"Why does it cost that much?" demanded Vi, forgetting the Italian flagman and his earrings, as Russ hurried her toward the car steps. "Are you sure about the third of a cent, Russ?"

Laddie looked back and waved his hand to the man who wore earrings. "Good-bye!" he called to the man.

"Good-a-bye!" cried the flagman in return, smiling very broadly. "Good-a-bye!"

"Why does he talk so funny?" asked Vi, panting, as Russ helped her up the car steps and into the vestibule.

"He talks broken English," said Russ in return. "Come on, Laddie."

Vi remembered that answer, and later, when she was helping Laddie relate the story of their adventure to Mother Bunker and daddy and the other children, she declared that the man with the earrings was "a broken Englishman," and would have it that Russ told her so.

It had been a very exciting time, both for the twins when they were lost and for the rest of the family on the train. Vi and Laddie could not stop talking about it. And, really, it had been a very important adventure in their small experience.

"That man with the earrings thought he knew us, too," Vi said finally.

"Of course he didn't know you," Rose observed.

"He thought we were Mrs. Bam—Bam—— Laddie, whose little boy and girl did that man think we were?"

Laddie did not understand her question at first; but finally he realized what Vi meant.

"Oh, I know! 'Bambinoes.' That was the name. He asked us about our being called 'Bambinoes.'"

"Oh, dear me!" laughed Mother Bunker. "That was his way of saying 'babies.' He called you babies in his mixture of languages."

"Is that the broken English for little boy and little girl?" scoffed Vi. "I guess that man doesn't know very much, even if he does wear earrings."

There was quite a celebration over the return of Vi and Laddie to the train, for the other passengers made a good deal of the two little lost Bunkers. A lady and gentleman made a little party for them that afternoon at their end of the car. There was milk bought in the buffet car, and cakes. But Mun Bun declared he wanted ice-water. Nothing else would satisfy his thirst.

The glasses brought from home were all in use at the time at the "party"; so somebody had to go with Mun Bun to the ice-water tank at the other end of the car and get him his drink.

"I'll go," said Margy. "I can reach the paper cups."

"Be careful and don't spill the water all over him," Mother Bunker said to her, and the two smallest Bunkers went to the end of the car on that errand.

Margy borrowed the porter's stool in the anteroom to climb up to the rack where the waxed-paper cups were kept. Those cups pleased Mun Bun greatly.

"Wouldn't they be nice to make dirt pies in, Margy?" suggested the smallest Bunker longingly. "And puddings. If we only had 'em when we were at home, wouldn't they be nice?"

"But we haven't any sand pile here," Margy pointed out. "So we can't make dirt pies in them."

"We can fill them with water. There's lots of water. You push that button again, Margy, and let some more water run."

"But you mustn't spill it on you. You know mother said you shouldn't," replied the little girl.

Margy was, however, quite as pleased with the wax-paper cups as Mun Bun was. When one cup was full, Mun Bun took it and set it carefully down on the floor. Then he reached for another. He actually forgot he was thirsty he was so much interested in filling and stationing the cups in a long line on the floor.

The porter had left his station in the anteroom and did not see what the two children were doing. And the rest of the Bunker family were so much engaged at the other end of the car they quite forgot Margy and Mun Bun for the time being.

"Get another! Get another, Margy!" Mun Bun kept saying.

Margy reached down the cups until there was not another one in the rack. And by that time the ice-water dripped very slowly from the faucet. The tank was just about empty.

"I guess we have got it all, Mun Bun," said the little girl. "They are all full."

"And I didn't spill a drop on me," declared the little boy virtuously. "So mother will say I am a good boy, won't she?"

Just what Mrs. Bunker might have said had she come upon the little mischief-makers we cannot know. For it was the colored porter who was first to discover what the smallest Bunkers were doing. He came back from the other end of the car, smiling broadly at Mun Bun and Margy when he saw them. The two stood to one side and looked rather seriously at the tall colored man. Somehow they felt that perhaps their play would not entirely meet his approval.

Suddenly Mun Bun saw where the pleasant colored man was about to step. He cried out:

"Oh, don't! Look out! All our puddin' dishes!"

"What's that, little boy?" demanded the porter.

"Look out! You'll splash——"

Margy tried to warn him too. But she was too late. The porter stepped right into the first of the filled waxed-paper cups, and then went plowing on, almost falling over them!

"My haid and body!" gasped the porter, stumbling on until he had overturned and stepped on the complete array of waxed-paper cups. "What you chilluns been a-doin' here, eh?"

"Now you spilled 'em," cried Mun Bun. "Look, Margy, how he's spilled 'em."

There could be no doubt of that fact. The passage was a-flood with ice-water! The porter was sputtering, and the two children were inclined to be somewhat tearful when Daddy Bunker came along to see what they were up to.

"These yere pestiferous chilluns!" exclaimed the colored man, trying to mop up the flood. "And dem cups was near 'nough to las' me clear to Texas."

"All right—all right, Sam!" rejoined Daddy Bunker, giving the colored man a generous tip. "You get some more cups and some more ice, and call it square. I expect I'd better tie a halter to each one of my children for the rest of the journey so as to keep track of them. I can't trust them out of my sight any more."

It was not quite as bad as that, although daddy was really annoyed by what Mun Bun and Margy had done. They were old enough to know mischief from play, and he told them so. Mun Bun looked pretty sober when he got back to the party.

"Aren't we going to get to that wanch-place pwetty soon, Muvver?" he asked Mrs. Bunker. "'Cause if we ain't, I'd rather go back home. There aren't any nice plays here on this train. And I'm tired of it."

"I suppose you are tired of it, dear," his mother said, taking him upon her lap. "We are all pretty tired of it. But after another night's sleep we shall be near our journey's end."

This news was eagerly received by all the little Bunkers. Even Russ and Rose were tired of traveling by train. After a certain time, riding in the steam cars grew very wearisome. The Bunker children were active by nature, and Russ liked to build things. He missed the attic and the woodshed at home.

The train rocked on into the Southwest, and while the children slept it covered several hundred miles. After they got up and were washed and dressed and had breakfasted, the bags were packed, for they did not expect to open them again until they reached Cavallo.

They stared out of the windows, watching the prairie country slide past, now and then passing small herds of cattle, as well as many little towns at which the train did not halt.

"I suppose Cowboy Jack will come with ponies and we'll all have to ride horseback," said Rose. "I don't know that I can stick on very well."

"You did at Uncle Fred's," Russ told her.

"But maybe I have forgotten how," his sister said doubtfully.

But Rose need not have worried about riding pony-back on this occasion. When the train stopped at Cavallo and they all got out there were no horses waiting for the Bunkers at all. The town did not look like a cattle-shipping place. And there was not a cowboy in sight!

CHAPTER XIII

A SURPRISE COMING

There was a nice-looking railroad station at Cavallo and some rather tall buildings in sight. There was a trolley line through the town, too, and the children saw the cars almost as soon as they alighted from the train. But they were all loudly wondering where the cow-ponies were, and the cowboys whom they had expected to see.

The little Bunkers, of course, did not know that nowadays even the cattle-shipping towns of the Great West are changed from what they were in the old times. Whether they are improved by the coming in of other business besides that connected with the raising of cattle, horses, and sheep is a question that even the Westerners themselves do not answer when you ask them. But, in any case, Cavallo had changed a good deal since the time Daddy Bunker had previously seen it.

"And what can we expect? The range bosses ride around in automobiles now because it is easier and cheaper than wearing out ponies. And I read only the other day," added Mr. Bunker, "of a Montana ranch where they hunt strays in the mountains from an airplane. What do you think of that?"

"Are you sure Mr. Scarbontiskil got your message, Charles?" asked Mrs. Bunker of daddy. "Perhaps we had better go to a hotel."

"Oh!" cried Laddie, "I want to go right out where the cows and horses are."

"So do I," said Russ. "A hotel isn't very different from a Pullman coach."

And they were all tired of that—even daddy and mother. But while they were discussing this point (the children rather noisily, it must be confessed) a big man in a gray suit came striding toward them, his hand outstretched and a broad smile upon his bronzed face. He wore a crimson necktie and a heavy gold watch-chain with a bunch of charms dangling from it, and a diamond sparkled in the front of his silk shirt. Russ and Rose noticed these rather astonishing ornaments, and although they thought the man very pleasant looking, they knew that he was not dressed as men dressed back home. At least, daddy would never have worn just such clothes and ornaments. But he did not look at all like a cowboy.

"I reckon this is Charlie Bunker!" exclaimed the man in a booming voice. "I'd most forgotten how you looked, Charlie. And is this the Missus?" and he smiled even more broadly at Mother Bunker.

"That's who we are," cried Mr. Bunker quite as jovially as the big man spoke. "And these are the six little Bunkers, Mr. Scarbontiskil."

"Oh! That's him!" whispered Rose to Russ. "And I know I never can say that name!"

The ranchman, however, at once put Rose and everybody else at their ease on that point. When he took off his broad-brimmed hat to make Mrs. Bunker a sweeping bow, he said:

"Don't put on any dog out here, Charlie. I've most forgotten the name I was handicapped with when I was born. Nobody calls me anything like that out here. Call me 'Jack'—just 'Cowboy Jack.' It fits me a sight better, and that's true. I was a cow-puncher long before I got hold of a lot of good Texas land and began to own mulley cows myself. Now, let me get acquainted with all these little shavers. What's their names? I bet they got better names than my folks could give me."

Rose and Russ, and even the smaller children, liked Cowboy Jack right away. Who could help liking him, even if he did shout when he spoke and wear such flashy clothes? His smile and his twinkling eyes would have won him friends in any company of children, that was sure. And then, though the clothes were odd, the children were not at all certain that they were not more beautiful than those their father wore.

And what a game they made of telling Cowboy Jack their names, so that he would remember them—"get 'em stuck in his mind" as he called it.

"I can remember 'Russ' because he is the oldest," declared Cowboy Jack. "And 'Rose' is the sweetest flower that grows, and I can't forget her. And 'Violet'? Why! she's the first blossom that comes up in the spring, and I sure couldn't forget her. And this boy, her twin, you say? 'Laddie'? Why, that's just what he is—a laddie. I couldn't mistake him for a lassie, so I'm sure to get his name stuck in my mind," and Cowboy Jack boomed a great laugh, shaking hands with each of the children as daddy presented them.

"And this is 'Margy,'" proceeded the ranchman. "I'd know that was her name just to look at her. She couldn't have any other name but 'Margy.' No other would fit. Now, that's all, isn't it?" added Cowboy Jack, his eyes twinkling very much as he looked right at Mun Bun but appeared not to see him. "Russ, and Rose, and Violet, and Laddie, and Margy? Yes, that must be all."

"There's me!" exclaimed the littlest Bunker, staring up at the big man.

"What's that I hear?" asked Cowboy Jack, looking all about the platform, and up in the air, and over the heads of the Bunker children. "Did I hear somebody speak?"

The five older Bunker children began to giggle, but Mun Bun did not take the matter as a joke at all. He was quite sure he was being overlooked and that he was just as important as anybody else in the crowd.

"Here's me!" cried Mun Bun again, and he laid hold of the skirt of Cowboy Jack's long coat and tugged at it. "You forgot me."

"Jumping grasshoppers!" exclaimed the big man, staring down at Mun Bun. "What do I see? Another Bunker?"

"It's me," said Mun Bun soberly. "I have a name, too."

"I—I wouldn't have seen you if you hadn't pulled my coat-skirt," declared the ranchman quite as soberly as the little boy himself. "And are you a Bunker? Honest?"

"I'm Mun Bun," said the little boy.

"Jumping grasshoppers!" ejaculated the ranchman, stooping down very low and staring at Mun Bun. "Another Bunker—and named 'Mun Bun'? That's a very easily remembered name, isn't it? I couldn't forget you—sure I couldn't! For you see every time I go to the bake shop I buy buns—and you are a bun, so you say. Are you a currant bun, or a cinnamon bun, or what kind of a bun are you?"

"I'm a Bunker bun," declared the little boy. "And you can't eat me."

"No, I can't eat you," admitted the ranchman. "But I can pick you up—this way—and carry you off, can't I?"

And he suited his action to the word and rose up with Mun Bun on one of his palms, and held him right out on a level with his twinkling eyes and smiling lips. Mun Bun squealed a little; but he liked it, too. It was just like being carried about by a giant!

The next thing was to get something to eat in the lunchroom of the railroad station. To be sure, breakfast had been not many hours before, but there was a long trip yet before Cowboy Jack's ranch would be reached, and one could always count on one or more of the six little Bunkers being hungry if not fed at rather frequent intervals. So sandwiches and buns—cinnamon buns, not Mun Buns—were bought, and milk for the children and coffee for the grown-ups, and a light lunch was eaten. There was really not very much to choose from, but the children were satisfied with what was got for them.

"Now, come on, all you little Bunkers," said Cowboy Jack. "We've got to start right away for my ranch, or we won't get there before supper time; and then Maria Castrado, my cook, won't give us anything but beans for supper."

"Oh! Where are your horses?" cried Laddie and Vi together.

"Out on the range," said Cowboy Jack. "Plenty of 'em there."

"But don't we ride out to your ranch on them?" Russ wanted to know, as Cowboy Jack strode around the railroad station, again carrying Mun Bun, and they all trooped after him.

"Got something that beats cayuses," declared Cowboy Jack. "What do you think of these for cow ponies?"

What he pointed out to them were two great, eight-cylinder touring-cars, both painted blue, and behind the steering-wheel of each a smiling Mexican who seemed as glad to see the Bunker children as Cowboy Jack was himself.

"Pile in! Pile in!" said Cowboy Jack in his great voice.

He gave Mun Bun over to Mrs. Bunker, who got into one car with daddy and the hand baggage. But he put all the other children into the tonneau of the other car and got in with them. It was quite plain that he was fond of children and proposed to have a lot of fun with the little Bunkers who had come so far to visit him.

"I've got a lot to show you youngsters," he said to Russ and the others when the cars started. "And I have a surprise for you out at my ranch."

"What is the surprise?" Vi asked. "Is it something we can eat? Or is it a surprise we can play with?"

"You can't eat my surprise," said Cowboy Jack, with one of his widest smiles. "But you can have a lot of fun with it."

"What is it?" asked Vi again.

"If I tell you now, it won't be a surprise," replied the ranchman. "So you'll have to wait and see it."

They drove through the town in the automobiles, and it seemed a good deal like an Eastern town after all. People dressed just the same as they did in Pineville and there was a five-and-ten-cent store painted red, and a firehouse with a motor-truck hook-and-ladder just like the one at home. Russ and Laddie thought maybe they would not have any use for their cowboy and Indian suits after all.

But by and by the motor-cars got clear of the town and struck into a dusty road on which there were no houses at all. In the distance Rose spied a moving bunch of cattle. That looked like a ranch; but Cowboy Jack told her that his ranch was still a good many miles ahead.

The little Bunkers liked riding in these big cars, for the Mexicans drove them very rapidly. The road was quite smooth and they kept ahead of the dust, except when they passed some other vehicle. The dust was very white and powdery, and Margy and Laddie began to sneeze. Then they grabbed each other's right little fingers, curling the fingers around each other.

"Wish!" cried Violet eagerly. "Make a wish—both of you."

"What—what'll I wish?" stammered Laddie excitedly.

"Oh, dear! Now you spoiled it," declared Vi. "Didn't he, Rose?"

"He can't make the wish after he has spoken," agreed the older sister. "No, Laddie; it is too late now."

Margy began to wave her hands and evidently wanted to speak.

"Did you wish, Margy?" asked Vi.

The smaller girl nodded vigorously. Cowboy Jack laughed very heartily, but Rose said to the little girl:

"You can talk now, Margy."

"I wished we'd have waffles for supper," announced Margy, hungrily. "I like waffles."

"And I bet we have 'em!" cried their host, laughing again. "Maria can make dandy waffles."

"Well, I would have wished for something—just as nice if you'd let me," Laddie broke in. "I don't see why I couldn't wish, even if I did speak first."

"That's something mighty mysterious," said the ranchman soberly. "We can't change the laws about wishing. That would bust up everything."

He talked so queerly that sometimes the little Bunkers were not sure whether he was in earnest, or only joking. But they all liked Cowboy Jack very much. And best of all—so Rose thought—they did not have to call him by his right name!

The sun was very low when the cars got into a winding road through a scrubby sort of wood and then climbed into the range of hills that they had been approaching for two hours. Mun Bun was asleep. But the children in the ranchman's car were all eagerly on the outlook for the first sight of the ranch houses which Cowboy Jack told them would soon appear.

"And then for the surprise," said Russ to Rose. "I wonder what it can be?"

"Something nice, I am sure," sighed his sister contentedly. "It must be something nice, or Mr. Cowboy Jack would not have mentioned it."

CHAPTER XIV

AN INDIAN RAID

It did seem, however, that the ranchman must have forgotten the surprise he had in store for the six little Bunkers. He was so busy getting his Mexican cook to make waffles for supper and seeing that the rooms had all been made ready by his Mexican house boys for the use of the Bunker family and doing a dozen other pleasant things for the comfort of his guests that he did not say a word about the surprise.

It had been almost dark when the party arrived at the broad, low house in which Cowboy Jack and his household lived. If the surprise was outside the house the children would have been unable to see it.

Mun Bun fell sound asleep over his supper, and Margy had to "prop her eyes open," as daddy declared, before the meal was done. Both these youngest Bunkers made no objection to going off to bed. But Vi and Laddie wanted to stay up as long as Russ and Rose did.

"We're almost as big as they are," declared Laddie, when he was questioned on this point. "And if Rose and Russ would only stop and wait for us a little, Vi and I would catch up to them—so now!"

But Russ and Rose were quite as eager to grow up as were Laddie and Vi; so they were not willing to wait, could they have done so. Daddy pointed out the fact of the "march of time" to the little folks and explained that everybody had to grow older each tiny second.

"Why can't we stop and wait?" demanded Vi. "We can stop an automobile and get out and wait."

"Or get lost from a train," put in Laddie, who was sitting on what Cowboy Jack called a "hassock"—a low seat—and studying a paper he had found. "I ought to make up a riddle about Vi and me being lost from the train that time."

"I'll give you a riddle," said Cowboy Jack, with one of his booming laughs.

"Is it a good one?" asked Vi.

"Please do!" cried Laddie. "I just love riddles."

"Well, here is one," said the ranchman. "'What is it that is black and white, but red all over?'"

"Black—white—and red?" repeated Laddie, puzzled, for if he had ever heard that riddle he had forgotten it.

"I know what is red, white and blue!" cried Vi. "That's the flag."

"Three cheers!" returned Cowboy Jack. "So you do, little girl. You've got the flag quite right. But this isn't the flag I am talking about."

"I don't believe I ever saw anything that was black and white but red, too," confessed Laddie slowly.

"Oh, yes, you have," said their big friend, apparently just as much entertained by the riddle as the little folks.

"I guess you must be mistaken, Mr. Cowboy Jack," said Laddie soberly. "I can't think of a single thing that is black and white, besides being red all over."

"Why, look at what you have in your hand!" exclaimed the ranchman.

"This is a paper," said Laddie.

"And isn't it black and white?"

"Yes, sir. The print is black and the paper is white. But I don't see any red——"

"But lots of us have read it all over," chuckled Cowboy Jack. "It is black and white, and is read all over!"

"Oh!" cried Laddie, clapping his hands, "that's another kind of 'red,' isn't it? I think that is a nice riddle. Don't you, Vi?"

But Vi was leaning against her mother's knee and her eyes were fast closed. She had gone to sleep in the middle of the talk about the riddle.

"It's time for all little folks to go to bed," said Mother Bunker.

So none of the six little Bunkers saw the surprise that night. But they had not forgotten it when morning came again. The six little Bunkers never forgot anything that was promised them!

While they were all at breakfast there was a great deal of noise outside—whooping and shouting and the like—that startled the children. But their mother would not let them leave the table to find out about it until breakfast was over. They heard, too, the pounding of ponies' hoofs, and then caught sight through the windows of a company of pony riders galloping by and off across the plain.

"Cowboys!" cried Russ. "I guess we'd better go back and put on our cowboy suits, Laddie."

The smaller boy was just as eager as Russ to get out and see the pony riders. As soon as they could honestly say they had eaten enough, Mother Bunker excused them all. But when they got outside upon the broad veranda at the front of the great house, the cowboys had disappeared.

There was something else in sight, however, that astonished the children more than the cowboys could, for they had expected to see them. Traveling across the plain some distance from the house was a procession that made all the little Bunkers shout aloud.

"What's those?" Rose asked at first sight. Rose almost always saw things first.

Russ gave one glance and fairly whooped: "Indians!"

"Oh, dear me!" gasped Rose, "are they wild Indians?"

"They are real Indians just the same!" exclaimed Russ, with confidence. "They aren't just the dressed-up kind. Look at them!"

The big Indians riding at the head of the procession wore great feather headdresses. "Feather dusters" Laddie called them. And they did look like feather dusters from that distance.

"We'd better get our guns and bows and arrows, hadn't we, Russ?" the little boy asked.

"The Indians are not coming this way," explained Russ. "I guess we're safe enough."

"See! There are Indian babies, too," cried Rose. "There's one strapped to a board on its mother's back—just like in the pictures."

"Just the same," said Vi, rather soberly for her, "I'm glad they are going the other way."

The Indians were traveling away from the ranch house and soon were out of sight. So before the children could ask any of the older people about them they were gone. And "out of sight out of mind" was almost always the rule with the little Bunkers, as daddy frequently said. Besides, there were so many new and interesting things to see that the matter of the Indians escaped the new-comers' minds.

There were great corrals down behind the big house, as well as bunkhouses in which the cowboys lived, and stables, and a long cook-shed in which three men cooked for the hands, as Cowboy Jack called his employees. Cowboy Jack owned a very large ranch and a great number of steers and horses and mules.

"It's almost like a circus," said Russ. "And all the different kind of dogs, too. That dog has hardly any hair, and he comes from Mexico, so they say. While that wolfy looking dog comes from away up in Alaska. Then there are dogs from places all between Alaska and Mexico."

This information he had gained from one of the Mexican boys with whom he became acquainted. They did not think to ask the friendly Mexican about the Indians, and not until the children went back to the house did they think to make inquiry about the procession they had seen right after breakfast. It was then Vi, inquisitive as usual, who broached the subject.

"Why do Indians wear feather dusters in their hair?" she asked.

"For the same reason that ladies wear feathers in their bonnets," declared Daddy Bunker seriously. "Because they think the feathers are ornamental."

"And why do they strap their babies to boards?" demanded Vi.

"Where did you see Indians?" asked Mother Bunker, guessing the source from which Violet's questions were springing.

"Oh!" cried Rose. "There were Indians—lots of them. We saw their parade go by—just like a Wild West Show parade."

Cowboy Jack began to laugh. And when he laughed his great body shook all over, and the chair in which he sat shook too.

"Are there Indians here, Mr. Scarbontiskil?" asked Mother Bunker.

"That's part of the surprise I told the children about," said Cowboy Jack, nodding to Mother Bunker, but smiling at the interested children. "Those Injuns are a part of it."

But he would not tell them any more—at least, not just then.

"It's a sort of a riddle," said Laddie eagerly, when they were all out of doors again. "I know it's a riddle. And we ought to find the answer."

"Well," scoffed Vi, his twin, "you can sit down and think of your old riddle if you want to. I'm going to pick flowers for mother."

"There must be some nice flowers here," agreed Rose. "I'll go look, too, Vi."

"Me want to pick flowers!" cried Mun Bun eagerly.

He always wanted to do anything the older children did. And picking flowers was one thing Mun Bun could do pretty well, little as he was. Holding a hand each of Rose and Vi he trudged off from the ranch house. Russ and Margy and Laddie came after. Russ and Laddie were still discussing the matter of putting on their cowboy suits so as to help herd the cattle with Cowboy Jack's "other hands." Just at this time, however, they became more interested in picking flowers.

For they did find pretty blossoms along the wagon track they followed. The ranch house was soon out of sight, for the children went over a little ridge and then down into a swale in which were clumps of low trees. It was quite a pretty country, and there was much to interest them.

At one place something jumped out of the shrub and went leaping away along the wagon track with great bounds.

"A rabbit!" cried Laddie. "Oh, such a big rabbit!"

"The very longest legs I ever saw," agreed Russ. "And long ears—like those on the mules in the corral."

"And he thumps the ground just like a horse stamping," said Rose. "There he goes out of sight. I—I believe I would be afraid of that rabbit if he came at me."

"Well, he is going, not coming," remarked Russ. "I want to see where he went."

He and Laddie started on the run to mount the little ridge over which the jackrabbit had disappeared. This ridge crossed the swale, or valley, and divided what lay beyond from the view of the six little Bunkers. When the children climbed the rise and came to the top, they all stopped. Even Russ did not say a word for a full minute; nor did Vi ask a question, so astonished was she by what she saw.

There, on the low land beside a stream of water, was a log cabin. It looked like a dilapidated cabin, for there were no windows and the door was off its leather hinges. There was a bonfire by the doorstep and a black kettle was hung over the fire from the tripod of smoke-blackened sticks.

On the doorstep sat a woman who appeared to be rocking her baby to sleep in her arms. She was watching whatever was cooking in the pot. A man was chopping wood a little way; from the doorstep. He wore a funny fur cap, with the tail of some animal hanging from it down to his shoulder, and his hair was tied in a funny looking queue—the strangest way for a man to dress his hair the little Bunkers had ever seen.

Suddenly Russ pointed behind the cabin—over to another ridge, or knoll, of land.

"Look!" Russ gasped. "Those Indians!"

None of the Bunker children had thought of the Indians they had seen as really wild Indians. But here came riding the Indian men now on active ponies, and with be-feathered spears in their hands. Their headdresses nodded, and, as the redmen rode nearer, the children saw that their faces were broadly striped in red and yellow. The paint made the Indians' faces look frightful.

"Oh!" cried Rose, clinging to Mun Bun, who clung to her in return. "Those Indians are coming right at that woman and her baby—and the man!"

"It's an Indian raid," murmured Russ. "Do you suppose it is real, or just make-believe?"

CHAPTER XV

A PROFOUND MYSTERY

Russ Bunker was a sensible chap, and it did not seem to him that the Indians could really mean to harm the people living in the old cabin. Cowboy Jack would not have let the children wander away from the ranch house unwarned had wild Indians been in the neighborhood.

At least, so Russ tried to believe. But the other little Bunkers were much frightened, and when the redmen began to hurry their horses down toward the cabin at the side of the stream, and began to whoop and yell and wave their be-feathered spears, even Rose turned back and began to run toward the ranch house.

"Come on, Russ! Come on!" she cried to her older brother. "That poor little baby!"

"Aw, I don't believe the Indians are really going to hurt those folks," objected Russ.

Nevertheless, he soon caught up with his sister and the others. Russ did not remain to see the outcome of the Indians' attack upon the cabin.

The younger children did not altogether understand what the excitement was all about. But they caught some fear from Russ and Rose and were willing to hurry along the wagon track without making objection at the pace the older children made them travel.

And here came another astonishing thing. Out of a woody place appeared a cavalcade of horsemen—and they were not cowboys! In fact, for a minute Russ and Rose were just as frightened as they had been by the charging Indians. Then Russ exclaimed, with a deal of relief:

"Oh, Rose! I know those men. They are soldiers!"

"All in blue clothes?" questioned Rose in doubt. "Soldiers don't wear blue clothes. They are dressed in khaki or olive-drab. Like Captain Ben was when he first came to our house."

"Those are soldiers. They have got swords and guns," repeated Russ confidently. "And I guess they are American soldiers, too."

"Well, they are not Indians, anyway," agreed Rose. "I guess they won't hurt us, anyway. We can go by 'em. Don't be afraid, Mun Bun."

"Not 'fwaid," declared the littlest Bunker. "But I want to see muvver and daddy."

"Sure you do," agreed Russ kindly. "Guess we all do. Come on. I'm going to tell that man riding ahead what the Indians are doing to those folks at the cabin."

They could still hear faintly the yells of the supposed savages behind the hill, down which the little Bunkers had just run. This noise did not seem to disturb the men in blue, who trotted their horses along the wagon track in a most leisurely manner.

The six little Bunkers stood off the track as the soldiers rode nearer. The chains on the horses' bits jangled, and the sun flashed from the barrels of the short guns and from the sword hilts. The men wore broad-brimmed hats with yellow cords around them, and one of the men riding ahead, who was an officer, wore a plume on the side of his hat.

"It's more than Indians that wear feather headdresses," whispered Vi to Rose. "So why do they?"

Like a number of Vi's other questions, this one remained unanswered. When the head of the procession came up Russ began to speak quite excitedly to the man leading it:

"Please, Mister Officer! There are Indians over that hill. Don't you hear them? And they are going to hurt some white people I guess."

"There's a baby," added Rose earnestly. "I wouldn't want the baby to be scalped."

"Hi!" exclaimed the leader of the soldiers, "it will be pretty tough if Props' rag baby gets scalped, that's a fact. Come on! Shack along, boys! They are looking for us now, I bet."

This seemed rather a strange way to command a troop of cavalry, and even Russ Bunker was puzzled by it. But as the soldiers in blue rode on at a faster pace Rose called after them:

"Please save the baby! Look out for the baby!"

"We'll do that little thing, girlie," promised one of the soldiers riding in the rear. "Don't you fear. We'll save the baby and the whole bunch!"

This was quite reassuring to Rose's troubled mind. But Russ was greatly puzzled. These soldiers did not look like the soldiers he had seen, nor did they act or speak like soldiers. He stared after them with great curiosity as they disappeared over the hill. But the other little Bunkers were so anxious to get back to the ranch house that Russ could not remain any longer to satisfy his curiosity.

Rose and the smaller children told the story about the Indians and the people at the cabin and about the soldiers in a very excited way to Mother Bunker. But Russ went to find Cowboy Jack. He felt that the ranchman should know all about what was going on in that valley, and about both the Indians and the soldiers in blue.

Mother reassured the younger Bunkers. There was nothing really to be afraid of, she told them. But she did seem mysterious and smiled a good deal while she was telling the children not to fear any of the strange things they might see about Cowboy Jack's ranch.

"It isn't anything like Uncle Fred's ranch," declared Laddie. "Why! it's a regular riddle here at Cowboy Jack's. I guess I can think how to ask that riddle in a minute—or maybe an hour. Let's see."

So Laddie—or the others—was not by when Russ propounded his question to Cowboy Jack, the big ranchman.

"Those Indians? I told you they were part of the surprise I had for you little Bunkers," declared Cowboy Jack, laughing very heartily.

"And the soldiers?" murmured the puzzled Russ.

"Part of the same surprise," answered the ranchman.

"We—ell, we were surprised. But I don't just understand how you come to have wild Indians and soldiers—and they don't look just like our soldiers back East—here on your ranch. And how about that baby?"

"I promise you," said Cowboy Jack quite seriously, "that the baby will not be scalped—or any of the white folks at all. Those Indians are not so savage as they seem. To-night, after the day's work is over, I'll take you over to the redskins' camp and you can get acquainted with them."

Russ was rather startled by this suggestion. He wanted to be grateful for anything that Cowboy Jack said he would do; but—but——

"Will Daddy Bunker go too?" asked Russ, suddenly.

"Sure. We'll take your daddy along with us," agreed Cowboy Jack.

"Then I'll go," said Russ Bunker, with a sigh.

He would go anywhere daddy went, although the matter of the wild Indians did seem to be a profound mystery.

CHAPTER XVI

MUN BUN TAKES A NAP

After lunch that day Mun Bun managed to have the most astonishing adventure of his life! And nobody could ever have imagined that the littlest Bunker could get into trouble just by falling asleep.

He had walked so far and seen so many strange sights that morning that after eating Mun Bun was just as sleepy as he could be. But he was getting old enough now to think that he should be ashamed of taking a nap in the afternoon.

"Only babies take naps, don't they, Muvver?" he said to Mother Bunker. "And I aren't a baby any more."

"You say you are not," agreed his mother quietly. "But of course you must prove it if we are all to believe that you are quite grown up."

"I'm growed too big to take naps, anyway," declared Mun Bun, quite convinced.

"What are you going to do if you grow sleepy?" asked his mother, before he started out after the other children.

"I'll pinch myself awake," declared Mun Bun. "Oh, I'll show I'm not a baby any longer."

He was some way behind the other children; but as he started in their wake Mother Bunker did not worry about him. She was confident that Russ and Rose would look out for the little boy, even if he was finally overcome with sleep.

But as it happened, the other little Bunkers had run off to see a lot of mule colts in a special paddock some distance from the big ranch house. Mun Bun saw them in the distance and he sturdily started out to follow them. He was no cry-baby ordinarily, and the fact that the others were a long way ahead did not at first disturb Mun Bun's cheerfulness.

But something else began to bother him almost at once. The wind had begun to blow. It was not a cold wind, although it was autumn. But it was a strong wind, and as it continued to come in gusts Mun Bun was sometimes almost toppled off his feet.

"Wind b'ow!" gasped Mun Bun, staggering against the heavy gusts. "Oh, my!"

That last exclamation was jounced out of him by something that blew against the little boy—a scratchy ball of gray weed that rolled along the ground just as though it were alive! It frightened Mun Bun at first. Then he saw it was just dead weeds, and did not bother about the tumble-weed any more.

But when he got to a certain wire fence, through which he was going to crawl to follow the other little Bunkers, the wind had buffeted him so that he lay right down to rest! Mun Bun had never tried to walk in such a strong wind before.

The wind blew over him, and the great balls of tumble-weed rioted across the big field. In some places, against stumps or clumps of brush, the gray mats of weed piled up in considerable heaps. Mun Bun watched the wind-rows of weed roll along toward his side of the field with interested gaze. He had never seen anything like those gray, dry bushes before.

His eyes blinked and winked, and finally drowsed shut. He had no idea of going to sleep. In fact, he had declared he would not go to sleep. So of course what happened was quite unintentional on Mun Bun's part. While Mother Bunker thought he was with the other children, they had no idea Mun Bun had refused to take his usual nap and had followed them from the house.

The mule colts in the paddock were just the cunningest things! Margy and Vi squealed right out loud when they saw them.

"And their cunning long ears flap so funny!" cried Rose. "Did you ever?"

"But their tails are not skinned down like the big mules' tails," objected Laddie.

"Oh, they'll shave those later. That is what they do to the big mules—shave the hair off their tails, all but the 'paint-brush' at the end," said Russ, who knew.

The children pulled some green grass they found and stuck it through the wires for the colts to pull out of their hands and nibble. Mule colts seemed even more tame than horse colts, and the children each "chose" a colt and named it, although the colts ran around in such a lively way that it was difficult sometimes to keep them separated in one's mind and, as Cowboy Jack said when he came along to see what the children were about, to "tell which from t'other."

"Let me see," he added, in his whimsical way. "I have to count and reckon up you little Bunkers every once in so often so as to be sure some of you are not strays. Let's see: There should be six, shouldn't there? One, two, three, four, five—— But there's only five here."

"Yes, sir," said Rose politely. "Mun Bun's taking a nap, I s'pose."

"He is, is he?" repeated Cowboy Jack, with considerable interest. "And where has he gone for his nap?"

"He is up at the house with mother," Russ said.

"Oh, no, he isn't," said the ranchman. "I just came from the house and Mrs. Bunker asked me particularly to be sure that Mun Bun was all right."

"Where is Mun Bun, then?" asked Vi.

"He's lost!" wailed Rose.

"Why, he didn't come down here with us," Russ declared.

"He started after you," said the ranchman, quite seriously now. "You sure the little fellow isn't anywhere about?"

He was so serious that Russ and Rose grew anxious too. The other little Bunkers just stared. Vi said:

"He's always getting lost—Mun Bun is. Why does he?"

"'Cause he's so little," suggested her twin. "Little things get lost easier than big things."

"That's sound doctrine," declared Cowboy Jack.

But he did not smile as he usually did when he was talking with the little Bunkers. He was gazing all around the fields in sight. He asked Russ:

"Which way did you come down here from the house, Son?"

Russ pointed. "Down across that lot where the bushes are all piled up."

"Come on," said Cowboy Jack. "We'd better look for him."

"Oh!" cried Margy suddenly, "you don't s'pose the Indians got him, do you?"

"Those Injuns wouldn't hurt a flca," declared the ranchman, striding away so fast up the slope that the children had to trot to keep up with him.

"Do the Indians like fleas?" asked Vi. "I shouldn't think they would. Our cat at home doesn't."

"I know a riddle about a flea," said Laddie, more cheerfully. A riddle always cheered Laddie. "It is: 'What is the difference between a flea and a leopard?'"

"Jumping grasshoppers!" exclaimed Cowboy Jack. "I should think there was a deal of difference—in their size, anyway."

"No, their size hasn't anything to do with it," said Laddie, delighted to have puzzled the big man.

"A leopard is a big cat," said Russ. "And a flea can only live on a cat."

"Pooh! That isn't the answer," declared Laddie. "I guess that is a good riddle."

"It sure is," agreed Cowboy Jack, still striding up the hill. "What is the difference between a flea and a leopard? It beats me!"

"Why," said the little boy, panting, "it's because—because a leopard can't change its spots, but a flea can. You see, the flea is very lively and jumps around a whole lot——"

"Can't a leopard jump?" demanded Vi.

"We—ell, that's the answer. Somebody told it to me. A leopard just can't change its spots—so there."

"I think that's silly," declared Vi impatiently. "And I want to know what has become of Mun Bun."

They all wanted to know that. They were too much worried about the littlest Bunker to laugh at Laddie's riddle. They went up to the fence and crept through an opening where the tumble-weeds had not piled up in great heaps as they had in many places along its length. The wind was still blowing in fitful gusts, and Laddie and Margy and Vi took hold of hands when they stood up in the field.

"Now, where can that boy be?" demanded Cowboy Jack in his big voice, staring all about again. "If he followed you children down this way——"

"Mun Bun! Oh, Mun Bun!" shouted Rose.

Russ joined his voice to hers, and they continued to call as they wandered about the brush clumps and the piles of dry weeds.

But no Mun Bun appeared! The ranchman looked very grave. Russ and Rose really became frightened. How could they go back to Mother Bunker and tell her that her little boy was lost on this great ranch?

Then Cowboy Jack began to shout Mun Bun's name. And how he could shout!

"Ye—ye—yip!" he shouted. "You—ee! Ye—ye—yip! Mun Bun! Mun Bun!"

Rose shut her ears tight with her fingers.

"My goodness!" she whispered to Russ, "Mun Bun must hear that—or else he has gone a very long way off."

But Mun Bun was not a long way off. He was quite near. And after Cowboy Jack had shouted a second time all the other Bunkers, and the ranchman himself, heard a small voice respond—Mun Bun's voice.

"Here I is!" said the small voice. "I'm here—here!"

"I'd like to know where 'here' is," cried Cowboy Jack in his great voice. "If Mun Bun's up in the air I don't see his aeroplane; and if he's dug himself in like a prairie dog I don't see the mouth of his hole. And to be sure he isn't in this field——"

"Oh, yes, he is!" exclaimed Russ Bunker, suddenly diving for a great heap of tumble-weed against the wire fence. "Anyway, here is his voice, Mr. Cowboy Jack."

"Bring out his voice and let's see it," commanded the big ranchman.

The others began to laugh at that, but Mun Bun did not laugh. He had not had his sleep out and did not like being waked up. The ranchman's loud shout had aroused the little fellow, and when he found himself under the heap of scratchy, sticky weeds he did not like that either.

But Russ pulled the weeds away in a hurry. The wind had rolled a great bunch of the dead weeds upon Mun Bun and had quite hidden him from sight.

"Like the Babes in the Wood," said Rose thoughtfully. "Only the robins covered them up with leaves."

"I'm not a baby," complained Mun Bun. "And robins didn't cover me. It was nasty old dry grass things, and they've got prickers on them."

Indeed, Mun Bun was not quite his happy self again until they took him back to the house and Mother Bunker took him into her lap for awhile. Margy stayed in the house with him, so the two smallest Bunkers did not go with Cowboy Jack and daddy to see the Indians, as the ranchman had promised Russ.

They all climbed into one of the big blue automobiles and Cowboy Jack drove the car himself. It was not a long way to go; but it was over the prairie itself, for there was no trail to the Indian encampment.

"I see the tents!" cried Rose, standing up in the back of the car to see over the windshield.

"Those are wigwams," said Russ. "Aren't they wigwams, Mr. Scarbontiskil?"

"You look out or my name will get stuck crossways in your throat and choke you," growled the ranchman. "You can call 'em wigwams. But those are just summer shacks, and not like the winter wigwams. Anyhow, up there on their reservation, these Indians have pretty warm and comfortable houses for the winter."

The children did not understand all of this, but they were very much interested and excited. When the car stopped before the group of tent-like structures a number of Indian children and women gathered around, laughing and talking. They seemed to be very pleasant people, and not at all like the wild-looking red riders the little Bunkers had seen earlier in the day.

"But I am just as glad those painted men are not here," Rose said to Russ. "Aren't you, Russ?"

But Russ had begun to see that there must be some trick in it. These squaws and Indian children would not be so gentle if their husbands and fathers were as savage as they had appeared to be. He could not exactly understand it, but there was a trick in it he was sure. Another surprise coming!

CHAPTER XVII

IN CHIEF BLACK BEAR'S WIGWAM

"Where is Black Bear, Mary?" asked Cowboy Jack of an old woman who was cooking something in a pot over one of the fires in the open.

"Out on the job, Mr. Jack," was the reply. "They ought to be in soon, for the sun is too low for good light. You can go into Bear's wikiup if you want to."

"Oh! A bear!" whispered Vi, clinging to daddy's hand. "Is it loose?"

"I expect it is loose, all right," chuckled daddy. "But you will probably not find it a very savage bear."

"Has it teeth—and claws?" pursued the little girl. "Bears bite, don't they?"

"I promise you that this one won't bite you," boomed Cowboy Jack's great voice. "He's just as tame a bear as ever you saw. Isn't he, Mary?"

The old woman smiled kindly at the children and nodded. She was old and wrinkled, and her face looked as though it had been cured in the smoke of many campfires. Nevertheless, she was a pleasant woman and even Vi felt some confidence in her statement. At least, all four little Bunkers went with Cowboy Jack and daddy to the big skin and canvas tent that stood in the middle of the camp. It was the biggest tent of all.

It was rather dark inside the tent; but Cowboy Jack had a hand-torch in his pocket, and he took this out and flashed the light all about the interior of the tent by pressing his thumb on the switch of the torch.

"Never know what you'll find in these Injun shanties," muttered Cowboy Jack. "Black Bear is college bred, but he's Injun just the same——"

"Goodness me! what does he say?" gasped Rose.

"Why, this Black Bear is a man!" exclaimed Russ. "He's an Indian. And I guess he must be a chief of the tribe. Is he, Daddy?"

"You've guessed it," laughed Daddy.

"Was he one of those awful painted Indians we saw riding down on the cabin?" queried Rose. "Are they safe?"

Daddy laughed and assured her that "out of business hours" the painted Indians were quite as gentle as the women and children about the camp.

But Rose and Russ could not just understand what the Indians' "business" could be. It was a very great mystery, and no mistake!

Vi and Laddie were so curious that they wished to examine everything in the wikiup. And there were many, many things strange to the children's eyes. Brilliant colored blankets hung from the walls, feather headdresses with what Vi called "trails," so that when a man wore one the tail of it dragged to his heels. There were beaded shirts and pretty moccasins and long-stemmed pipes decorated with beads and feathers in bunches. There were, too, little skins and big skins hanging from the framework of the Indian tent, and most of the floor was soft with cured wolf hides, the hair side uppermost.

"Black Bear is 'heap big chief,'" chuckled Cowboy Jack. "When he travels he takes a lot of stuff with him. Hello! Here they come, I reckon."

The four small Bunkers heard the pounding of the ponies' hoofs on the plain. They peered out of the "door" of the wikiup as daddy held back the blanket that served as a curtain over the entrance.

"Oh, they are the painted Indians!" wailed Vi, and immediately hid her face against Rose's dress.

"They won't hurt you," scoffed Laddie. "You know they won't with daddy and Mr. Cowboy Jack here."

"But—but what did they do to that woman at the cabin—and her baby?" wondered Vi with continued anxiety.

"I don't see any scalps," said Laddie confidently. "Maybe it isn't the fashion to scalp folks any more out here."

"You can ask Black Bear about that," chuckled Cowboy Jack. "I'm not up in the fashions, as you might say."

The big ranchman was evidently vastly amused by the little Bunkers' comments. The four children peered out of the wikiup and saw the party of horsemen dismount. A tall figure, with a waving headdress, came striding toward the children. Vi and Laddie, it must be confessed, shrank back behind the ranchman and daddy.

"Hullo!" exclaimed Cowboy Jack. "Here's Black Bear now."

"But he doesn't look like a bear," Laddie whispered. "Bears don't walk on their hind feet."

"Sometimes they do," said Daddy Bunker. "And this Bear does all the time. He is 'Mr. Bear' just the same as my name is 'Mr. Bunker.'"

The tall man lifted off his headdress and handed it to one of the women who came running to help him. Underneath, his hair was not like an Indian's at all—at least, not like the Indians whose pictures the Bunker children had seen. Black Bear's hair was cut pompadour, and if it had not been for the awful stripes across his face he would not have looked bad. Even Rose admitted this, in a whisper, to her brother Russ.

It was interesting for the four little Bunkers to watch Black Bear get rid of the paint with which his face was smeared. He stripped off the deerskin shirt he wore and squatted down on his heels before a box in the middle of the tent—a box like a little trunk. When he opened the cover and braced it up at a slant, the children saw that there was a mirror fastened in the box lid.

The Indian woman held a lantern, and Black Bear dipped his fingers in a jar of cold-cream and began to smear his whole face and neck. He looked all white and lathery in a moment, and he grinned in a funny way up at Cowboy Jack and Mr. Bunker.

"Makes me think of the time they cast me for the part of the famous Pocahontas in the college play of 'John Smith,'" said Black Bear. "That was some time—believe me! We made a barrel of money for the Athletic Association."

"Oh!" murmured Rose, "he talks—he talks just like Captain Ben—or anybody!"

"He doesn't talk like an Indian, that's so," whispered back Russ, quite as much amazed.

But Violet could not contain her curiosity politely. She came right out in the lantern-light and asked:

"Say, Mister Black Bear, are you a real Indian, or just a make-believe?"

"I am just as real an Indian, little girl, as you ever will see," replied the young chief, still rubbing the cream into his face and neck. "I'm a full-blood, sure-enough, honest-Injun Indian! You ask Mr. Scarbontiskil."

"But you're not savage!" said the amazed Vi. "Not as savage as you all looked when you were riding down on that cabin to-day. We saw you and we ran home again. We were scared."

"No. I'm pretty tame. I own an automobile and a talking-machine, and I sleep in a brass bed when I'm at home. But, you see, I work at being an Indian, because it pays me better than farming."

"Oh! Oh!" gasped Laddie. "Scalping people, and all that?"

"No. There is a law now against scalping folks," said Mr. Black Bear, smiling again. And now that he had got the yellow and red paint off his face his smile was very pleasant. "We all have to obey the law, you know."

"Oh! Do Indians, too?" gasped Rose.

"Indians are the most law-abiding folks there are," declared the chief earnestly.

"Then I guess I won't feel afraid of Indians again," confessed Rose Bunker. "Will you, Russ?"

But Russ did not answer. He felt that there was a trick about all this. He could not see through it yet; but he meant to. It was worse than one of Laddie's riddles.

By and by Chief Black Bear got all the paint off his face. Then he washed the cold-cream off. He pulled on a pleated, white-bosomed shirt, and buttoned on a collar and tied a butterfly tie in place. Then he went behind a blanket that was hung up at one side of the wikiup, all the time talking gaily to Cowboy Jack and Mr. Bunker, and when he reappeared he was dressed just as Daddy Bunker dressed back home when he went to the lodge or to a banquet!

The four little Bunkers stared. They could not find voice for any comment upon this strange transformation in Black Bear's appearance. But Cowboy Jack was critical.

"Some dog that boy puts on, doesn't he, Charlie?" he said to Mr. Bunker. "He thinks he's down in New Haven, or somewhere, where he went to college. Beats me what a little smatter of book-learning will do for these redskins."

This did not seem to annoy Chief Black Bear at all. He laughed and slapped the big ranchman on the shoulder.

"Of course I'm a redskin—just as you are a whiteskin. Only I have improved my opportunities, Jack, while you have allowed yourself to deteriorate." That last was a pretty hard word, but Russ and Rose understood that it meant "fall behind." "Probably your grandfather had a college education, Jack," went on the Indian chief. "But your father and you did not appreciate education. My father and grandfathers, away back to the days of LaSalle and even to Cortez's followers who marched up through Texas, had no educational advantages. I appreciate my chance the more."

"But a boiled shirt and a Tuxedo coat!" snorted Cowboy Jack.

"Keeps me a 'good Indian,'" laughed Black Bear. "No knowing how savage I might be if I didn't dress for dinner 'most every night."

Russ knew all this was joking between the chief and the ranchman, and he saw that Daddy Bunker was very much amused. But the boy did not understand what the Indians were doing here in Cowboy Jack's ranch, and why they should dress up like wild savages in the daytime, and then dress in civilized clothes when evening came.

Russ Bunker had never been more puzzled by anything in his life before. He felt, of course, that Daddy Bunker would explain if he asked him; but Russ liked to find out things for himself.

CHAPTER XVIII

THE NEW PONIES

Out of a box Chief Black Bear took certain treasures that he gave to the four little Bunkers who visited his wikiup. He even sent some fresh-water mussel shells, polished like mother-of-pearl, to the absent Margy and Mun Bun, of whom Cowboy Jack told him.

"They are some nice kids," declared the ranchman, who sometimes used expressions and words that were not altogether polite; but he meant no harm. "Especially that Mun Bun. He went to sleep in a fence-corner to-day and got covered up with tumble-weed. But he's an all right boy."

Cowboy Jack seemed to think a great deal of the smallest of the Bunkers. He was frequently seen admiring Mun Bun. Even the other children noticed it, and Rose had once asked her mother:

"Why doesn't Mr. Scar—Scar—well, what-ever-it-iskil! Why doesn't he have children of his own?"

"But, my dear, everybody cannot have children just for the wishing," Mother Bunker replied.

"I should think he could," murmured Rose. "See how many children these Indians and Mexicans have; and they are none of them half as nice as Mr.— Mr.—well, Mr. Cowboy Jack."

To Russ and Rose and Laddie and Violet, Black Bear gave stone arrow-heads which may have been used by his forefathers when they roamed the plains, wild and free, as the young Indian said. But better than those, he gave Rose and Violet little beaded moccasins that fitted just as though they were made for the little white girls!

The children went away after that, for it was time for their own supper at the ranch house and Cowboy Jack always seemed afraid of making Maria Castrada cross if they were late for meals. But perhaps it was his own hearty appetite that spurred him to be on time.

At any rate, the Bunkers left Chief Black Bear sitting cross-legged before a low table on which the Indian women were serving his dinner, beginning with soup and from that going on through all the courses of a properly served meal.

"Funny fellow, that Black Bear," said Cowboy Jack to Mr. Bunker. "But maybe he's got it right. I was brought up pretty nice—silverware and finger-bowls, and all that sort of do-dads; but part of my life I've lived pretty rough. Black Bear has set himself a certain standard of living, and he's not going to slip back. Afraid of being a 'blanket Indian,' I suppose."

The children—even Russ and Rose—did not understand all this; but they had been much interested in Chief Black Bear.

"Only, I don't see why he paints up in the daytime and rides such wild ponies, and all that," grumbled Rose, who, like Russ, did not like to be mystified.

Whenever they tried to ask the older folks to explain the mystery they were laughed at. It was Cowboy Jack's mystery, anyway, and Mr. and Mrs. Bunker did not feel that they had a right to explain to the children all that they wished to know.

"Figure it out for yourselves," said Daddy Bunker.

"Is it a riddle, then?" demanded Laddie. "It must be a riddle. Why does Chief Black Bear paint his face, and—and——"

"And take it off with cold cream?" put in Vi. "Why does he?"

"I guess that's the riddle," said her twin. "You answer it, Vi."

But although Vi could ask innumerable questions on all sorts of subjects she seldom was able to answer one—and certainly not this one Laddie propounded.

Next morning while the six little Bunkers were at the big breakfast table in Cowboy Jack's ranch house there again arose a considerable disturbance outside in front of the house. This time the children were pretty well over their meal, and they grew so excited that Mother Bunker allowed them to be excused.

Russ and Rose led the way out upon the veranda. There stood two of the smiling Mexican houseboys—"cholos," Cowboy Jack called them—and they bade the Bunker children a very pleasant good morning. Russ and Rose did not forget their manners, and they replied in kind. But the four smaller children just whooped when they saw what had brought the Mexicans to the front of the big house.

One of the men led two saddled ponies while the other held another fat pony that drew a brightly painted cart with seats in it and a step behind—just the dearest cart! Rose Bunker said.

"Oh, I know I can learn to drive that dear, dear pony!" Rose added. "And there is room for every one of you children with me in the cart."

"Huh!" exclaimed Laddie. "I am going to ride pony-back like Russ does. Which is my pony, Mr. Cowboy Jack?" he asked of the ranchman who had followed them out of the house to enjoy their amazement and delight.

"The one with the shortest stirrups, I guess," Russ said. "This one looks as if I could ride him," and he took the bridle handed him by the Mexican.

"Oh, lift me up! Lift me up!" cried Laddie, running to the other saddle pony.

Cowboy Jack strode down and did so. Meanwhile Rose and the other children were scrambling into the pony-cart, while the pony which drew it tossed its head and looked around as though counting the number of passengers that were getting aboard.

"Isn't he just cute?" cried Rose again. "Oh, Mr. Cowboy Jack! you are so good to us."

"Got to be," said the ranchman, laughing. "I haven't any little folks of my own, so I have to treat those I find around here pretty well, I do say."

Laddie clung to both the pommel and the bridle-reins at first, for he did seem so high from the ground at first. But Russ trotted away on his pony very securely. Russ had ridden quite a little at Uncle Fred's ranch and had not forgotten how.

Rose decided that she liked better to drive. But Vi must learn to drive, too, she said. And even Margy and Mun Bun clamored to hold the reins over the back of the sleepy brown pony. Russ's mount was what Cowboy Jack called a pinto, but Russ said it was a calico pony. He had seen them marked that way before—in the circus. Laddie's pony was all white, with pinkish nose and ears. Right at the start Laddie called him "Pinky." But the little girls could not agree on a name for the pony that drew their cart.

There seemed to be so many nice names that just fitted him! Margy wanted to call him Dinah after her lost doll.

"But that Dinah-doll was black," said Rose, in objection. "And this pony is brown. Maybe we ought to call him Brownie."

"Oh! I know!" cried Vi. "Let's call him Cute. He's just as cunning as he can be."

But this name did not appeal to the others, and they were no nearer finding a name for the brown pony when the ride was over and they all came back to the ranch house than at first. They had had so much fun, however, that they had forgotten for the time being the mystery of the Indians and soldiers whom they had seen the day before.

Laddie had thought up a new riddle—and it was a good one. He knew it was good and he told everybody about it, he was so excited.

"Listen!" he cried, when he half tumbled out of his saddle by the steps of the veranda. "This is a good riddle. Listen!"

"We're listening, Son," said Cowboy Jack. "Shoot!"

"What is it," asked Laddie earnestly, "that looks like a horse, has four legs like a horse, runs like a horse, eats like a horse, but it isn't a horse?"

"A cow," said his twin promptly.

"No, no! A cow has horns. A horse doesn't," Laddie declared scornfully.

"A colt," guessed Russ.

"No, no!" rejoined the eager Laddie. "A colt is a little horse, so that could not be the answer, Russ Bunker."

"A giraffe," suggested Vi again.

"I wish you wouldn't, Vi," complained the riddle-maker. "Does a giraffe look like any horse you ever saw?"

"A carpenter's horse," said Rose.

"Pooh! That's made of wood. Can a wooden horse run?" cried Laddie.

"I guess that is a pretty good riddle," said Russ soberly. "What is the answer, Laddie?"

"Do you all give it up?" asked the smaller boy, his eyes shining.

"You got us thrown and tied," declared Cowboy Jack solemnly. "I couldn't guess that riddle in a thousand years."

"But you wouldn't want to wait that long to know what it is," Laddie said delightedly. "Now, would you?"

"You'd better tell us now, Laddie," said Daddy Bunker smilingly. "You know a thousand years is a long time to wait."

"Well," said the little fellow proudly, "what looks like a horse, and has four legs like a horse, and runs like a horse, and eats like a horse, is——"

"Yes, yes!" exclaimed the impatient Violet.

"What is it, Laddie?"

"Why," said Laddie, with vast satisfaction, "it is a mule."

They all cried out in surprise at this answer. But it was a good riddle.

"Only," said Russ thoughtfully, "it's lucky you didn't say anything about its tail and ears. Then we would have caught you."

The Bunker children had so much fun with the ponies Cowboy Jack had selected for their use during the next two or three days that they thought of very little else. The mystery of the Indians and soldiers did not often trouble their minds. But something else did. Mail came from the East, and with it was a letter from Captain Ben, and another from Norah.

"And," said Mother Bunker soberly, reading the letters to the children, "both say that they have found neither Rose's wrist-watch nor Laddie's stick-pin. I am afraid, Rose and Laddie, that your carelessness has cost you both your jewelry. It is too bad. But perhaps it will teach you the lesson of carefulness with your possessions."

This, however, did not make either Rose or Laddie feel any better in their minds. They had been very proud of both the lost articles and it looked now as though they would never see the watch and the pin again.

CHAPTER XIX

RUSS BUNKER GUESSES RIGHT

One morning, while Mother Bunker was amusing the four younger children in the house (for the twins and Margy and Mun Bun could not always go where Rose and Russ went) the two older Bunker children rode away from the big ranch house on that very wagon-trail that had led them into such a strange adventure the first day of their stay on Cowboy Jack's ranch. Rose rode on Laddie's pony, Pinky.

Russ and Rose had thought of something the night before, and they had planned this ride in order to do it. They had remembered Black Bear's wild Indians and the strange soldiers in blue. The two older Bunker children decided to try to find those strange people again, and the man and woman and baby at the brookside.

Just who those "white settlers" could be, and why they were living in that part of the ranch away from Mr. Cowboy Jack's nice house, neither Russ nor Rose had been able to make up their minds. Of course, there was a mystery about it, and a mystery was bound to worry the little Bunkers a good deal. They were persistent, and Russ, at least, seldom gave up any problem until he had solved it.

"I saw a picture in a big book at the ranch," said Rose to her brother, "and in it a frontiersman—that's what the book called him—was dressed like that man we saw chopping wood—the man with the squirrel-tail on his cap and his long hair tied in a queue."

"Did you? But that must have been the way they wore their hair a long, long time ago."

"It said in the book under the picture that trappers and hunters out West here wore their hair long and tied in queues long after they stopped doing so anywhere else. Some of the white hunters wore a scalp-lock like the Indians. I guess maybe that was a scalp-lock," said Rose.

"Well, those soldiers——"

"They are not dressed like soldiers are now," Rose interrupted. "But in the book there were pictures of soldiers in the Mexican War—When was that, Russ?"

Russ had read a little American history in his class the term before and thought he knew something about the Mexican War. He told Rose it had been fought long after the Revolution.

"Well, the pictures showed soldiers in the Mexican War dressed like those we saw the other day. Or, anyway, very much like them."

"Goodness me!" exclaimed Russ, "don't you suppose these soldiers know that war is over?"

So they had started out without saying anything to the older folks about their real object. In the first place, Russ and Rose did not like to be laughed at. And they knew that Cowboy Jack, at least, was very much amused by the fact that the little Bunkers had not guessed the mystery of the Indians and soldiers now on his ranch.

The brother and sister rode on through the valley they had traveled before and up to the top of the ridge from which they had seen the cabin by the side of the stream. The cabin was now in truth deserted. There was no fire before it and not a person in sight.

"Maybe those Indians took them captive. The poor little baby!" murmured Rose.

"Don't be a little dunce, Rose!" exclaimed Russ, with exasperation. "You know that nice Black Bear would not hurt them. And, anyway, I guess that baby was only a doll. That is what that soldier said when you told him about it. He said it was Mr. Props' rag baby."

"Who do you suppose Mr. Props is?" asked Rose. "And Mrs. Props? It must have been Mrs. Props we saw holding the—er—baby. For maybe it was a real baby."

Russ saw there was no use in arguing on this point. He urged his calico pony forward and Pinky followed promptly. The two Bunkers went along the trail past the cabin and up the next slope. They struck into a woodsy sort of road then, and by and by the children saw that the trail was leading them to a ravine between two steep hills. There was much shrubbery, so they could not see very clearly what was before them, but as they continued to ride on there came suddenly a lot of noise from the ravine. Horses whinnied, men shouted, and two or three guns were discharged.

"Oh! It's a fight, Russ!" shrieked Rose. "Do come away!"

But Russ had seen something that interested him very much. Among the bushes on one side of the ravine he saw several Indians creeping. They wore feathers in their scalp-locks, and had bows and arrows and guns. He did not see Black Bear with this company of Indians, but they were acting just as though they were fighting somebody down in the bottom of the ravine.

"It's an—an ambush, Rose!" cried Russ excitedly. "Oh! There's a man with a machine——"

In fact he saw two men with boxes on tripods, standing side-by-side and not many yards away in the trail. The men were turning cranks on the sides of the boxes.

Another man turned and saw the Bunker children apparently riding nearer. He started back toward them, shouted and waved his arms.

"Oh, dear me!" shrieked Rose. "It's—it's dynamite! They are going to blow up something! Come, Russ!"

She twitched at Pinky's bridle, and the pony swerved about and plunged away at such a fast pace that poor Rose could only cling to the bridle and saddle and cry. But Russ remained where he was. He was greatly amazed, but slowly a comprehension of the whole thing was forming in the boy's mind.

"It's—it's only make-believe," Russ Bunker told himself. "They are not doing anything dangerous. It's a—a play, that's what it is. Why, those men have got moving picture cameras!

"Oh, I know what the surprise is now—Mr. Cowboy Jack's surprise! It's a moving picture company!" said Russ Bunker aloud. "They are make-believe soldiers, even if Black Bear and his people are real Indians. They are making moving pictures—that is what they are doing, Rose."

But when he turned in his saddle to look for Rose, the girl and Pinky had completely disappeared.

"My goodness!" said Russ, somewhat alarmed, "she's so frightened that she has run back home. Maybe she will fall off the pony."

Much as he would have liked to remain to watch the actors and the Indians make the picture on which they were at work, Russ felt it his duty to see that Rose was all right. If anything happened to Rose daddy and mother might blame Russ, because he was the oldest.

The pinto pony cantered away with Russ at quite a fast pace. He kept to the wagon-trail that led back to Cowboy Jack's ranch house. And at every turn Russ expected to see Pinky and Rose ahead.

But he did not see his sister on Laddie's pony. He came in sight of the big house, and even then he did not see her. So, when the pinto stopped before the big veranda and Mother Bunker and the other children appeared, Russ could scarcely find voice enough to ask:

"Oh, Mother! have you seen Rose? Did she come back alone?"

"Rose? I have not seen her since you both rode away together. Do you mean to say——" Then Mother Bunker saw that Russ was having hard work to keep back the tears and she—wise woman that she was—knew that this was no time to scold the boy.

"Where did she go? When did you lose her?" his mother cried, running down the steps.

"Back—back where they are making the moving picture," gasped Russ. "She was scared by the Indians shooting at the whites. But, of course, they were only making believe. And—and Rose rode away somewhere and—and—oh, Mother! I can't find her."

CHAPTER XX

PINKY GOES HOME

Rose had seen men digging and blasting at home in Pineville for the new sewer system; so when the moving picture man had run back toward her and Russ to warn them not to get into the field of the camera, Rose had thought a charge of dynamite was about to be exploded.

Although the man who warned them did not wave a red flag, dynamite was all Rose could think of. The appearance of the Indians on the hillside, in any case, frightened her, and she was quite ready to yield to panic. As we have seen, she twitched Pinky, the pony, around by his bridle-rein, and the spirited pony proceeded to gallop away.

Rose did not pay any attention to where Pinky was going. And Pinky did not remain on the trail by which the brother and sister had traveled from Cowboy Jack's ranch.

Pinky was very anxious to go, but where he went he did not care. He left the trail almost at once and cantered through a pasture where the scattered clumps of brush and greasewood soon hid him and his rider from the sight of anybody on the wagon-trail. At least, they were quite hidden from Russ Bunker when he rode back to look for his sister.

Rose did not at first worry at all about where she was or where Pinky was taking her. She listened for the expected "boom!" of the dynamite explosion. But as minute after minute passed and the explosion did not come, Rose began to wonder if she had made a mistake.

Pinky kept right on moving, just as though he knew where he was going and wished to get there shortly. But when Rose looked around she knew she had never been in this place before. And, too, she discovered that Russ had not followed her.

This last discovery made Rose pull up the pony and think. It alarmed her. She was not often frightened when Russ was by, although she had given way to fright on this particular occasion. But she knew she would not have been afraid had her brother been right here with her.

As it was, Rose was very much frightened indeed. She did not know where Russ was, nor did she know where she was. Therefore it was positive that she was lost!

Now, Pinky was a very intelligent pony, as was afterward proved. You will read all about it later. But he could not know that Rose wished him to find his way home unless she told him as much. And that Rose did not do.

She just burst out crying, and the pony had no idea what that meant. He turned to look at her, tossed his head and pawed with one dainty hoof. But he did not understand of course that the girl on his back was crying because she was lost and was afraid.

Perhaps, too, if Rose had let the bridle-reins alone Pinky would have remembered the corral and his oats and have started back without being told that the ranch house was the thing Rose Bunker most wanted to see. But the little girl thought she had to guide the pony; so she grabbed up the reins at last and said:

"Come up, Pinky! We have just got to go somewhere. Go on!"

Pinky naturally went on the way he was headed, and that chanced to be in a direction away from Cowboy Jack's home, where the Bunkers were then visiting. Nor did the pony bear her toward the place where the moving picture company was at work.

They went on, and noon came, and both Pinky and the little girl were hungry and thirsty.

Pinky smelled water—or saw it. He insisted on starting off to one side of the narrow trail they had been following.

Rose was afraid to leave that trail, for it seemed to her that a path along which people had ridden enough to make a deep rut in the sward must be a path that was more or less used all the time. She expected to meet somebody by sticking to this path, or else come to a house.

But here was a shallow stream, and Pinky insisted on trotting down to it and wading right in.

The water was cool, and the pony cooled his feet in it as well as his nose. He had jerked the reins out of Rose's hands when he had sunk his nose in the water, and she had no way of controlling him.

"You bad, bad Pinky!" cried Rose, leaning down, clinging with one hand to his mane and reached with the other hand to seize the reins. But she could not reach them. She lost her stirrups. She slipped forward off the saddle and upon the pony's neck.

At this Pinky was startled. He tried to scramble out of the brook. He stepped on a stone that rolled. And then he staggered and half fell and over his head and right into the middle of the brook flew Rose Bunker! It was a most astonishing overturn, to say nothing of the danger of it.

Splash went Rose into a pool of water! But worse than getting wet was the fact that one of her ankles came in contact with a stone, and the pain of the hurt made Rose scream aloud. Oh, that knock did so hurt the little girl!

"Now! Now see what—what you've done!" cried Rose, when she could speak. "You naughty, naughty Pinky!"

Pinky had snorted and run a few steps up the bank. Now he was grazing contentedly—not trying to run away from the little girl at all, but quite inconsiderate of her, just the same. He let Rose sit on the edge of the brook, with her hurt foot in the water, crying as hard as she could cry, and he acted as though he had no interest in Rose at all!

At least, he acted this way until he had got his fill of grass. Then he trotted back to the brook for another drink. He did not come very near Rose, who had crawled up out of the water and sat rocking herself too and fro and nursing her hurt ankle. It was so badly wrenched that the little girl could not bear her weight upon that foot. She had tried it and found out "for sure."

Otherwise she might easily have caught Pinky, for the pony was tame enough in spite of his being spirited. But she could not walk far enough to catch the pony; and then she could not have jumped up into the saddle.

Pinky got tired of looking at her, perhaps. Anyway, after drinking again he wandered up from the brook and once more fell to grazing. But he was not hungry now, and he remembered the corral at the ranch house. Besides, something moved behind a clump of brush and startled him.

The pony threw up his head and snorted. His ears pointed forward and he looked questioningly at the clump of brush. The creature behind the bushes moved again, and at that Pinky dashed away, whistling his alarm. Rose saw him go, but she could not stop him. And fortunately, for the time being, she did not know what had frightened the pony and sent him off at so quick a pace. He disappeared, and with his going it seemed to Rose that her last thread of attachment to the big ranch house and Daddy and Mother Bunker was broken.

When Pinky was out of sight and sound Rose stopped crying. In fact, she stood up and did try to hobble a few steps after him. For Rose was wise enough to see that the pony had probably started for home, and in that same direction lay her best path too.

But she really could not limp far nor fast. The clumps of brush soon hid the pony, as we have said. And then poor Rose heard the same sound in the scrub that Pinky had heard!

"Oh! what is that?" breathed the little girl.

She had not thought of any danger from wild animals before this time, for it was broad daylight. And what this thing could be——

Then she caught a glimpse of it! It was of a sunburned yellow color, and it slunk behind a bush and seemed to be crouching there, hiding, quite as much afraid of Rose as Rose was of it. She saw its dusty tail flattened out on the ground. But whether it was frightened or was preparing to charge out upon her, the little Bunker girl could not tell and was greatly terrified.

She was just as frightened, indeed, as all the people at Cowboy Jack's ranch house were when Pinky, the runaway pony, cantered into view with nobody on his back. Cowboy Jack and daddy were already mounted on ponies, and Russ had refused to remain at home. He wanted to aid in the search for Rose.

"I can show them just where we were when Rose turned back," he said to Mother Bunker. "And then Cowboy Jack ought to be able to follow Rose."

"I hope so," agreed his mother.

Then she, as well as the little folks, shouted aloud at the appearance of the cantering Pinky.

"He's thrown the girl off!" exclaimed the ranchman. "Or else she has tumbled off. And it was some time ago, too. Come on, Charlie Bunker! I'm going to get Black Bear and his Injuns to help us look for her."

"Oh, Mr. Scarbontiskil!" murmured Mrs. Bunker, "is there anything out there in the wilderness to hurt her—by day?"

"Not a thing, Ma'am—not a thing bigger or savager than a jackrabbit," declared Cowboy Jack.

"But I wonder where the pony left her?" queried Mr. Bunker.

"Ask him, Daddy—ask him," urged Laddie eagerly. "He's an awful intelligent pony."

Pinky had been halted before the group at the ranch house. Daddy Bunker said again:

"I wonder if he could show us where he left Rose?"

And when he spoke Pinky began to nod his head up and down and paw with one hoof. The children were delighted—even Russ.

"Oh! I believe he is trying to explain," Russ cried. "Ask him another question, Daddy."

Mr. Bunker laughed rather grimly. "Let Vi ask the pony questions; she can think of them faster than I can. Or let Laddie ask him a riddle. There is no time to experiment with ponies now."

He and Cowboy Jack started away from the ranch house, and Russ, for fear of being left behind, urged his pinto after them.

He felt very much frightened because of Rose's absence. And he felt, too, as though it might be his fault, although none of the older people had suggested such a thing. Still, Russ knew that he ought to be beside his sister right now!

CHAPTER XXI

THE LAME COYOTE

Rose had, of course, heard of coyotes. She had heard them talked about here at Cowboy Jack's ranch. But she had not caught a glimpse of one before. Nor did she know this slinking creature behind the bushes was that animal which ranchmen consider such a pest.

Although coyotes are very cowardly by nature and will seldom attack human beings, even if starving or enraged, the beasts do kill young calves and lambs and raid the ranch hen-houses just as foxes do in the East.

Besides, on the open range, the coyotes howl and whine all night, keeping everybody in camp awake; so the cowboys have a strong dislike for Mr. Coyote and have not a single good word to say for him. Indeed, the coyote seems to possess few good traits.

But Rose Bunker called the creature that had startled her a dog.

"If I could run I know that dog would chase me!" she sobbed. "I wonder who it belongs to? It must be a runaway dog, to be away out here where there are no houses. I'm afraid of that dog."

For this Rose was not to be much blamed. This was a strange country to her, and almost everything she saw was different from what she was used to back in Pennsylvania. Even the trees and bushes were different. And she never had seen a dog just like that tawny one that dragged itself behind the hedge of bushes.

The strange part of it was—the thing that frightened Rose most—was that the animal seemed trying to hide from her. And yet she felt that it must be dangerous, for it was big and had long legs. She was quite right in supposing that if she had undertaken to run, under ordinary circumstances, the animal could have overtaken her.

But Rose's ankle throbbed and ached, and she cried out whenever she rested that foot upon the ground. She just couldn't run! So she began cajoling the supposed dog, hoping that it was not as savage as she really feared it was. One thing, it did not growl as bad dogs often did, as Rose Bunker very well knew.

"Come, doggy! Nice doggy!" she cooed. And then she was suddenly afraid that it really would come! If it had leaped up and started toward Rose the little girl would have fallen right down—she knew she would!

But the yellow-looking creature only tried to creep farther under the scrubby bushes. Rose began to think that maybe it was more afraid of her than she was of it.

"Poor doggy!" she said, hobbling around the end of the hedge of scrubby bushes.

There she saw its head and forepaws. And it was not until then that she discovered what was the matter with the coyote. Its right fore paw was fast in a steel trap. A chain hung from the trap. It had broken the chain and hobbled away with the trap—no knowing how far it had come.

"The poor thing!" Rose said again, at once pitying the coyote more than she was afraid of it.

Yet when it saw the little girl looking at him it clashed its great jaws and grinned at her most wickedly. It was not a pleasant thing to look at.

"But he is hurt, and 'fraid, I suppose," Rose murmured. "Why! he's just as lame as I am. I guess his foot hurts him in that awful trap a good deal more than my ankle hurts me. The poor thing!"

The coyote was evidently quite exhausted. It probably had come a good way with that trap fastened to its paw. But it showed Rose all its teeth, and they did look very sharp to the little girl.

"I would not want him to snap at me," thought Rose. "And if I went near enough I guess he would snap. I'll keep away from the poor dog, for I would not dare try to get the trap off his foot."

She moved away; but she kept the crouching coyote in sight. She did not like to feel that it was following her without her seeing it do so. And the coyote seemed to feel that it wanted to keep her in sight. For it raised its head and watched her with unwinking eyes.

This incident had given Rose something to think about besides her own lost state and her lame ankle. The latter was not paining as badly as at first. Still, she did not feel that she could hobble far. And she was not quite sure now in which direction Pinky, the pony, had run. She really did not know which way to go.

"It is funny Russ didn't come after me," thought the little girl. "Maybe those Indians got him. But, then, there was the white man. I thought he was setting off dynamite. But there wasn't any explosion. I guess I ran away too quick. But Russ might have followed me, I should think."

She could not quite bring herself to blame her difficulties on Russ, however, for she very well knew that her own panic had brought her here. Russ had been brave enough to stay. Russ was always brave. And then, she had blindly ridden off the trail and come to this place.

"I guess I won't say Russ did it," she decided. "It wouldn't be so. And I expect right now he is hunting for me, and is worried 'most to death about where I am. And daddy—and Mother Bunker! I guess they will want to know where I've got to. This—this is just dreadful. Maybe I shall have to stay here days and days! And what shall I ever eat, if I do? And I haven't even any bed out here!"

The lost girl felt pretty bad. It seemed to her, now that she thought more about it, that she was very ill used. Russ did not usually desert her when she was in trouble. And Rose Bunker felt that she was in very serious trouble now.

She sat down again in plain view of the lame coyote and cried a few more tears. But what was the use of crying when there was nobody here to care? The lame coyote had its own troubles, and although it watched her, it did not care a thing about her.

"He is only afraid I might do something to hurt him," thought Rose. "And I wouldn't do a thing to hurt the poor doggy. I wonder if he is thirsty?"

The stream of water into which Rose had tumbled from Pinky's back was only a few yards away, and perhaps the wounded coyote had been trying to get to it before the little girl and the pony came to this place. But the animal was too wary to go down to drink while Rose was in sight. And fortunately there was nothing Rose could take water to the coyote in. For she certainly would have tried to do that, if she could. She was just that tender-hearted.

But it would have been unwise, for the coyote's teeth were as sharp as they looked to be, and it would not have understood that the little girl merely wished to help.

Rose sat and watched the beast, and the lame coyote crouched under the bushes and watched her, and it grew into mid-afternoon. Rose felt very sad indeed. She did not see how she could walk back to the ranch house, even if she knew the way. And she could not understand why Russ did not come for her.

Meanwhile Russ was urging his pinto pony as fast as he could after Cowboy Jack and Daddy Bunker. They followed the regular wagon-track through the valley and over the ridge which had now become quite familiar to the little boy. They passed the cabin by the stream and then came to the knoll from which that morning Russ and Rose had seen the moving picture cameras.

But neither those machines nor the men who worked them nor the Indians on the hillside were now in sight. Cowboy Jack, however, seemed to know just where to find the moving picture company, for he kept right on into the ravine.

"I reckon this is about where you saw the Indians and the camera men, Son?" the ranchman said to Russ.

"Yes, sir," said Russ. "But Rose left me right on this hill. I thought she went back——"

"I didn't notice any place where she left the trail," interposed Cowboy Jack. "But I reckon Black Bear can find where she went. You have to hand it to those Injuns. They can see trailmarks that a white man wouldn't notice. And going to college didn't spoil Black Bear for a trail-hunter."

"He is quite a wonderful young man," Daddy Bunker said.

But Russ was only thinking about his sister. He wondered where she could have gone and what had happened to her. Pinky's coming back to the ranch alone made Russ believe that something very terrible had happened to his sister.

He urged his pinto pony on after the ranchman and daddy, however, and they all entered the ravine. It was a very wild place—just the sort of place, Russ thought, where savage Indians might have lain in wait for unfortunate white people. He was very glad that Black Bear's people were quite tame. At least, they could not be accused of having run away with Rose.

In a few minutes Cowboy Jack had led them up through the ravine and out upon what he called a mesa. There were patches of woods, plenty of grass that was not much frost-bitten, and a big spring near which a number of ponies were picketed. There was a traveling kitchen, such as the Army used in the World War. Men in white caps and jackets were very busy about the kitchen helping the moving picture company to hot food.

And the actors and Indians were all squatting very pleasantly side by side eating and talking. The Indians wore their war-paint, but they had drawn on their shirts or else had blankets around their shoulders. Russ saw Black Bear almost at once. He stood talking with some of the white men—notably with the one who was the commander of the soldiers, the man with the plume in his hat.

But it seemed that a little man sitting on a campchair off to one side and talking to a man who had a lot of papers in his hands was the most important person in view. It was to this man that Cowboy Jack led the way.

"That is Mr. Habback, the director," Russ heard the ranchman tell daddy. "We must get him to let us have Black Bear, or somebody."

The next moment he hailed the moving picture director.

"Can you spare some of your Injuns for an hour?" asked Cowboy Jack. "There's a little girl lost, and I reckon an Injun can find her trail better than any of my cholos or punchers. How about Black Bear?"

The young Indian whose name he had mentioned came towards the group at once. Mr. Habback looked up at Chief Black Bear.

"Hear what this Texas longhorn says, Chief?" he said to the Indian. "A little girl lost somewhere."

"I can show you about where she left the trail," explained the ranchman earnestly.

"Was she over at my wikiup the other evening?" asked Black Bear, with interest.

"She—she's my sister," broke in Russ anxiously. "And she was scared by your Indian play, and the pony must have run away with her."

"Hullo!" said Chief Black Bear. "I remember you, too, youngster. So your sister is lost?"

"Well, we can't find her," said Russ Bunker.

"I will go along with them, Mr. Habback," said the Indian chief, glancing down at the director. "I'll take Little Elk with me. You won't need us for a couple of hours, will you?"

"It's all right," said the director. "Go ahead. We can't afford to lose a little girl around here, that is sure."

"You bet we can't," put in Cowboy Jack. "Little girls are scarce in this part of the country."

Black Bear spoke to one of his men, who hurried to get two ponies. The Indians leaped upon the bare backs of the ponies and rode them just as safely as the white people rode in their saddles. This interested Russ a great deal, and he wondered if Black Bear would teach him how to ride Indian style.

But this was not the time to speak of such a thing. Rose must be found. For all they knew the little girl might be in serious trouble—she might be needing them right then!

The two Indians and the ranchman and Daddy Bunker started back through the ravine. None of them was more worried over Rose's disappearance than was Russ. He urged his pinto pony after the older people at the very fastest pace he could ride.

CHAPTER XXII

A PICNIC

Rose had now been so long alone that she was beginning to fear she never would see Mother Bunker and daddy and her brothers and sisters again. And this was an awful thought.

But she had already cried so much that it was an effort for her to squeeze out another tear. So she just sat on a stump and sniffed, watching the lame coyote.

Rose pitied that coyote. If he was as thirsty as she was hungry, the little girl feared the poor animal must be suffering greatly. For it was long past noon and breakfast at the ranch house was served early.

"I guess I'll have to begin to eat leaves and grass," murmured Rose Bunker. "I suppose I can wash them down with water, and there is plenty of water in the brook. Only the poor, doggy can't get to it."

While she was thinking these things, and feeling very miserable indeed, she suddenly heard the ring of horses' hoofs on the stones in the brook. Rose sprang up in great excitement, for she did not know what this new trouble might be.

Then——

"Oh, Daddy Bunker! Russ!" she shrieked, and began to hobble toward the cavalcade that had ridden down from the other side of the stream of water.

"Rose!" cried daddy. "Are you hurt, child?"

"Well, I was hurt. But my foot's pretty near well now. Only Pinky ran away and left me after I tumbled out of the saddle—Oh! Wait! Look out and don't scare off the poor lame doggy."

This last she cried when she looked back at the coyote trying to scramble farther into the bushes. But the chain hitched to the trap had caught over a stub, and the poor brute could not get far. Cowboy Jack drew from his saddle holster the pistol he usually carried when he was out on the range; but Rose screamed out again when she saw that.

"Don't hurt the poor doggy, Mr. Cowboy Jack! He can't get away."

"Jumping grasshoppers!" muttered the ranchman, "does she think that coyote is a dog?"

"She evidently does," Black Bear replied. "He can't get away. I'll tell Little Elk to stay back and fix him. No use scaring the child. Lucky the brute was fast in that trap. He might have done her harm."

Rose did not hear this, but Russ did. And he was quite old enough to understand his sister had been in danger while she remained here near the coyote. Besides, it would have been cruel to have left the wounded animal to die miserably alone. He could not be cured, so he would have to be shot.

This incident of the coyote made a deeper impression upon the mind of Russ than it did on his sister's. He quite understood that, had the animal been more savage or had it been free of the trap, it might have seriously injured Rose. There were perils out here on the open ranges that they must never lose sight of—possibilities of getting into trouble that at first Russ Bunker had not dreamed about. It made Russ feel as though never again would he let any of the younger children go anywhere alone while they remained at Cowboy Jack's.

Rose prattled a good deal to Daddy Bunker about the "lame dog" as they all rode back to the ranch house. But Russ was more interested in hearing about the moving picture company's camp and what they were doing. Black Bear told the little boy some things he wished to know, including the fact that the Indians and the other actors were making a picture about olden times on the plains, and that it was called "A Romance of the Santa Fé Trail."

"I should think it would be a lot of fun to make pictures," Russ said. "Do you think we Bunkers could get a chance to act in it, Chief Black Bear?"

"I don't know about that," laughed the Indian. "I shall have to ask Mr. Habback, the director. Maybe he can use you children in the scene at the old fort where the soldiers and frontiersmen are hemmed in by the Indians. Of course, there were children in the fort at the time of the attack."

"It—it isn't going to be a real fight, is it?" asked Russ, rather more doubtfully.

"It has got to look like a real fight, or Mr. Habback will not be satisfied, I can tell you."

"But suppose—suppose," stammered Russ, "your Indians should forget and really turn savage?"

"Not a chance of that," laughed Black Bear. "I have hard enough work making them take their parts seriously. They are more likely to think it is funny and spoil the shot."

"Then they don't ever feel like turning savage and fighting the white folks in earnest?" asked Russ.

"You don't feel like turning savage and fighting red men do you?" asked Black Bear, with a serious face.

"Oh, no!" cried Russ, shaking his head.

"Then, why should we red people want to fight you? You will be perfectly safe if you come down to see us make the fort scene," the Indian chief assured him.

So Russ got back to the ranch house full to the lips with the idea of acting in the moving picture. Rose's ankle had only been twisted a little, and she was perfectly able to walk the next day. But Mother Bunker would not hear to the children going far from the house after that without daddy or herself being with them.

"I believe our six little Bunkers can get into more adventures than any other hundred children," she said earnestly. "To think of that coyote being there with Rose for hours!"

"If he had not been in the trap he would have run away from her fast enough," returned Daddy Bunker.

Just the same he, too, felt that the children would better not get far out of their sight. They could play with the ponies about the house, for the fields were mostly unfenced. And the ponies were certainly great play-fellows. Laddie was sure that Pinky was a most intelligent horse.

"If we had known just how to talk to him," declared Laddie, "I am sure he would have told us all about Rose and where he had left her that day."

"Maybe he would," said Rose, though she spoke rather doubtfully. "But I slipped right out of that saddle, and I am not going to ride him any more. I would rather drive Brownie hitched to the cart."

"You mean Dinah, don't you?" asked Margy.

"I guess she means Cute," said Vi.

"Oh, no! Oh, no!" cried Mun Bun. "Let me name that pony. I want to call him Jerry. I want to call him after our Jerry Simms at home in Pineville."

And this was finally agreed upon. All the Bunker children liked Jerry Simms, who had been the very first person to tell them stories about the army and about this great West that they had come to.

"I guess Jerry Simms would have known all about this moving picture the soldiers and Mr. Black Bear's Indians are making," Russ remarked. "And mayn't we all go and act in it, Daddy?"

Russ talked so much about this that finally Mrs. Bunker agreed to go with the children to see the representation of the Indian attack on the fort. The six little Bunkers looked forward to this exciting proposal for several days, and when Mr. Habback sent word that the scene was ready to "shoot," as he called it, the children could scarcely contain themselves until the party started from the ranch house.

It was to be a grand picnic, for they took cooked food and a tent for Mother Bunker and the children to sleep in. Russ and Laddie rode their ponies, and all the rest of the party crowded into one of Cowboy Jack's big blue automobiles when they set out for a distant part of the ranch.

"I know we'll have just a bully time," declared Russ Bunker. "It will be the best adventure we've ever had."

But even Russ did not dream of all the exciting things that were to happen on that picnic.

CHAPTER XXIII

MOVING PICTURE MAGIC

It was rather rough going for the big car, and the little Bunkers were jounced about a good bit. Russ and Laddie trotted along on their ponies quite contentedly, however, and did not complain of the pace. But Vi began to ask questions, as usually was the case when she was disturbed either in mind or body.

"Daddy, why do we jump up and down so when the car bumps?" she wanted to know. "You and mother don't bounce the way Mun Bun and Margy and Rose and I do. Why do we?"

"Because you are not as heavy as your mother and I. Therefore you cannot resist the jar of the car so well."

"But why does the car bump at all? Our car at home doesn't bump—unless we run into something. Why does this car of Mr. Cowboy Jack's bump?"

"The road is not smooth. That is why," said her father, trying to satisfy that thirst for knowledge which sometimes made Violet a good deal of a nuisance.

"Why isn't this road smooth?" promptly demanded the little girl.

"Jumping grasshoppers!" ejaculated the ranchman, greatly amused, "can't that young one ask 'em, though?"

At once Vi's active attention was drawn to another subject.

"Mr. Cowboy Jack," she demanded, "why do grasshoppers jump?"

"Fine!" exclaimed Daddy Bunker. "You brought it on yourself, Jack. Answer her if you can."

"That's an easy one," declared the much amused ranchman.

"Well, why do they jump?" asked the impatient Vi.

"I'll tell you," returned Cowboy Jack seriously. "They jump because their legs are so long that, when they try to walk, they tumble over their own feet. Do you see how that is?"

"No-o, I don't," said Vi slowly. "But if it is so, why don't they have shorter legs?"

"Jump—Never mind!" ejaculated Cowboy Jack. "You got me that time. I reckon I'll let your daddy do the answering. You fixed me, first off."

So Vi never did find out why grasshoppers had such long legs that they had to jump instead of walk. It puzzled her a good deal. She asked everybody in the car, and nobody seemed able to explain—not even Daddy Bunker himself.

"Well," murmured Vi at last, "I never did hear of such—such iggerance. There doesn't seem to be anybody knows anything."

"I should think you'd know a few things yourself, Vi, so as not to be always asking," criticized her twin.

Daddy Bunker was much amused by this. But the next moment the wheels on one side of the car jumped high over a clod of hard earth, and daddy had to grab quick at Mun Bun or he might have been jounced completely out of the car.

"What are you trying to do, Mun Bun?" demanded daddy sharply.

"I'm flying my kite," answered the little fellow calmly. "But I 'most lost it that time, Daddy."

Before getting into the automobile Mun Bun had found a large piece of stiff brown paper and had tied a string of some length to it. Although there was no framework to this "kite," the wind caused by the rapid movement of the automobile helped to fly the piece of paper at the end of the string.

"Look out you don't go overboard," advised Daddy Bunker.

"You hold on to me, Daddy—p'ease," said the smallest Bunker. "You see, this kite pulls pretty hard."

Russ and Laddie were riding close behind the motor-car, but on the other side of the trail. The minute after Mun Bun had made his request, a gust of wind took the kite over to that side of the car and it almost blew into the face and eyes of Russ Bunker's pony.

MUN BUNS' "KITE" FRIGHTENED THE PINTO. MUN BUNS' "KITE" FRIGHTENED THE PINTO.

Six Little Bunkers at Cowboy Jack's. (Page)

The pinto was very well behaved; but this paper startled him. He shied and wheeled suddenly to get away from the annoying kite. Instantly Russ shot over the pony's head and came down asprawl on the ground!

As he flew out of the saddle Russ uttered a shout of alarm, and Pinky, Laddie's mount, was likewise frightened. Pinky started ahead at a gallop, and Laddie was dreadfully shaken up. He squealed as loud as he could, but he managed to pull Pinky down to a stop very soon.

"Wha—what are you doing, Russ Bunker?" Laddie wanted to know. "Is that the right way to get off a pony?"

Russ had not lost his grip of the bridle-reins, and he scrambled up and held his snorting pony.

"You know I don't get off that way if I can help it," said Russ indignantly.

"But you did," said Laddie.

"Well, I didn't mean to. My goodness! but my knee is scratched."

The automobile had stopped, and Mother Bunker called to Russ to ask if he was much hurt.

"Not much, Mother," he replied. "But make Mun Bun fly his kite somewhere else. My pony doesn't like it."

"Mun Bun," said Daddy Bunker seriously, "I think you will have to postpone the flying of that kite until later."

"He'd better," chuckled Cowboy Jack, starting the car again. "First he knows he'll scare me, and then maybe I'll run the car off the track."

Of course that was one of Cowboy Jack's jokes. He was always joking, it seemed.

At last they came in sight of the place where the several big scenes of the moving picture were going to be photographed. A river that the little Bunkers had not before seen flowed here in a great curve which Cowboy Jack spoke of as the Oxbow Bend. It was a grassy, gently sloping field, with not a tree in sight save along the edge of the water.

Nevertheless, many trees had been brought here and a good-sized stockade, or "fort," had been erected. The structure was in imitation of those forts, or posts, of the United States Army that marked the advance of the pioneers into this vast Western country a good deal more than half a century ago.

Daddy Bunker had told the children something about the development of this part of the United States the evening before, and Russ and Rose, at least, had understood and remembered. But just now they were all more interested in the people they found here at the Oxbow Bend and in what they were doing.

In one place were several covered wagons and the traveling kitchen. Here the white members of the moving picture company lived. At the other side was the encampment of Black Bear and his people. The Indian camp had been brought to this place from the spot where the little Bunkers had first visited it.

Black Bear and Little Elk and the other Indians welcomed the little Bunkers very kindly. And on this occasion the Eastern children became acquainted with the little Indians who had come down from the Indian reservation in Oklahoma with their parents to work for the moving picture company.

Rose and Russ felt they knew these Indian boys and girls already. You see, they had seen more of the Indians than the other Bunker children had. They found that Indian boys and girls played a good deal like white children. At least, the dark-faced little girls had dolls made of corncobs and wood, with painted faces, and they wrapped them in tiny blankets. One little girl showed Rose her "best" doll which she had carefully hidden away in a tent. This doll was a rosy-cheeked beauty that could open and shut her eyes, and must have cost a good deal of money. She told Rose that Chief Black Bear had given the doll to her for learning Sunday-school texts.

The boys took Russ and Laddie down to the edge of the river and sailed several toy canoes that the men of the tribe had fashioned for them. The canoes were just like big Indian canoes, with high prows and sterns and painted with targets. Besides these toys the Indian boys had bows and arrows that were modeled much better than the bows and arrows Russ and Laddie owned, and could shoot much farther.

When Russ tried the Indians' bow and arrows he was surprised at the distance he could drive the arrow and how accurately he sent it.

"I guess you boys know how to make 'em right," he told Joshua Little Elk, one of the Indian lads and a son of the big Little Elk who had helped find

Rose when she was lost. "Laddie and I have only got boughten bow-arrows, and the arrows don't fly very good."

"My papa made this bow for me," said Joshua, who was a very polite little boy with jet-black hair. "And he scraped the arrows and found the heads."

The heads were of flint, just such arrow-heads as the ancient Indians used to make. But the modern Indians, if they used arrows at all in hunting, have steel arrow-heads which they buy from the white traders.

These things and a lot more Russ and Laddie learned while they were with the Indians. But there was not time for play all of the day. By and by Mr. Habback, the moving picture director, shouted through his megaphone, and everybody gathered at the stockade, or fort, and he explained what was to be done. Some of the pictures were to be taken that day; but the bigger fight would be made the day following.

However, the Bunker children were not altogether disappointed at this time. There was a run made by one of the covered wagons for the fort, and the little Bunkers, dressed in odds and ends of calico and sunbonnets and old-time straw hats, sat in the back of the wagon and screamed as they were told to while the six mules that drew the wagon raced for the fort with the Indians chasing behind on horseback.

Mun Bun might have fallen out had not both Russ and Rose clung to him. And the little fellow did not like it much after all.

"My hair wasn't parted, Muvver," he said afterward to Mother Bunker. "And I didn't have my new blouse on—or my wed tie. I don't think that will be a good picture of me. Not near so good as the one we had taken before in the man's shop that takes reg'lar pictures."

But although Mun Bun did not care much for the picture making, the other little Bunkers continued to be vastly amused and interested. They watched Black Bear and the commander of the soldiers smoke the pipe of peace in the Indian encampment. Mr. Habback allowed Russ to dress up like a little Indian boy to appear with Joshua Little Elk in this picture, because they were about the same size. They brought the ornamented pipe to the chief after it had been filled by the old Indian woman, Mary.

It was a very interesting affair, and if Mun Bun was bored by it, he fell asleep anyway, so it did not matter. But the next day the big fight was staged, and that was bound to be exciting enough to keep even Mun Bun awake. The fight was about to start and the call was made for all the children to gather inside the stockade.

The Bunkers were all to be there. But suddenly there was a great outcry around the tent that had been set up for the use of Mother Bunker and the six little Bunkers.

Mun Bun was not to be found. They sent the other children scurrying everywhere—to the soldiers' camp, to the Indian encampment, and all around. Nobody had seen Mun Bun for an hour. And in an hour, as you and I know, a good deal can happen to a little Bunker!

CHAPTER XXIV

MUN BUN IN TROUBLE

"Why does he do it, Daddy?" asked Vi.

"Why does he do what?" returned her father, who was too excited and anxious to wish to be bothered by Vi's questions.

"Mun Bun. Why does he?"

"Don't bother me now," said her father. "It is bad enough to have Mun Bun disappear in this mysterious way——"

"But why does he disappear—and everything?" Vi wanted to know. "He's the littlest of all of us Bunkers, but he makes the most trouble. Why does he?"

"I'm sure," said Mother Bunker, who had overheard Vi, "you may be right. But I can't answer your question and neither can daddy. Now, don't bother us, Vi. If you can't find your little brother, let us look for him."

The whole party at the Oxbow Bend was roused by this time, and men, women and children were looking for the little lost boy. Some of the cowboys who were working with the moving picture people scurried all around the neighborhood on pony back; but they could see nothing of Mun Bun.

Russ and Rose had searched everywhere they could think of. Mun Bun had not been in their care at the time he was lost, and for that fact Russ and Rose were very thankful. This only relieved them of personal responsibility, however; the older brother and sister were very much troubled about Mun Bun's absence.

The smallest Bunker really had succeeded in getting everybody at Oxbow Bend very much stirred up. Even the usually stolid Indians went about seeking the little white boy. And Mun Bun was nearer the Indians just then than he was to anybody else!

The little fellow had gone wandering off after breakfast while almost everybody else was down at the fort listening to Mr. Habback's final instructions about the big scene that was to be shot. Mun Bun had already expressed himself as disapproving of the picture. He knew he would not look nice in it.

He came to the Indian encampment, and the only person about was an old squaw who was doing something at the cooking fire. She gave Mun Bun no attention, and he looked only once at her. She did not interest the little boy at all.

But there was something here he was curious about. He had seen it before, and he wanted to see in it—to learn what the Indians kept in it. It was a big box, bigger than Mother Bunker's biggest trunk, and now the lid was propped up.

Mun Bun did not ask the old woman if he could look in it. Maybe he did not think to ask. At any rate, there was a pile of blankets beside the box and he climbed upon them and then stood up and looked down into the big box.

It was half filled with a multitude of things—beaded clothing, gaily colored blankets, feather headdresses, and other articles of Indian apparel. And although there was so much packed in the box, there was still plenty of room.

"It would make a nice cubby-house to play in," thought Mun Bun. "I wonder what that is."

"That" was something that glittered down in one corner. Mun Bun stooped over the edge of the box and tried to reach the glittering object. At first he did not succeed; then he reached farther—and he got it! But in doing this he slipped right over the edge of the box and dived headfirst into it.

Mun Bun cried out; but that cry was involuntary. Then he remembered that he was where he had no business to be, and he kept very still. He even lost interest in the thing he had tried to reach and which had caused his downfall.

Of a sudden he heard talking outside. It was talking that Mun Bun could not understand. He was always alarmed when he heard the Indians speaking their own tongue, for he did not know what they said. So Mun Bun kept very still, crouching down there in the box. He would not try to get out until these people he heard went away.

Just then, and before Mun Bun could change his mind if he wanted to, somebody came along and slammed down the lid of that box!

Poor little Mun Bun was much frightened then. At first he did not cry out or try to make himself heard. But he heard the person outside lock the box and then go away. After that he heard nothing at all for a long time.

Perhaps Mun Bun sobbed himself to sleep. At least, it seemed to him when he next aroused that he had been in the box a long, long time. He knew he was hungry, and being hungry is not at all a pleasant experience.

Meanwhile the search for the smallest Bunker was carried on all about the Oxbow Bend. In the brush and along the river's edge where the cottonwoods stood, and in every little coulee, or hollow, back of the camps.

"I don't see," complained Rose, "why we Bunkers have to be losing things all the time. There was my wrist-watch and Laddie's pin. Next came Vi and Laddie. Then Mun Bun was lost in the tumble-weed. Then I got lost myself. Now it's Mun Bun again. Somehow, Russ, it does seem as though we must be awful careless."

"You speak for yourself, Rose Bunker!" returned her brother quite sharply. "I know I wasn't careless about Mun Bun. I didn't even know he needed watching—not when daddy and mother were around."

Nobody seemed more disturbed over Mun Bun's disappearance than Cowboy Jack. The ranchman had set everybody about the place to work hunting for the little boy, and privately he had begun to offer a reward for the discovery of the lost one.

To Cowboy Jack came one of the older Indian men. He was not a modern, up-to-date Indian, like Chief Black Bear. He still tied his hair in a scalp-lock, and if he was not actually a "blanket Indian" (that is, one of the old kind that wore blankets instead of regular shirts and jackets), this Indian was one that had not been to school. Russ and Rose were standing with Cowboy Jack when the old Indian came to the ranchman.

"Wuh! Heap trouble in camp," said the old Indian in his deep voice.

"And there's going to be more trouble if we don't find that little fellow pretty soon," declared the ranchman vigorously.

"Bad spirits here. Bad medicine," grunted the old Indian.

"What's that? You mean to say one of those bootleggers that sell you reds bad whisky is around?"

"No. No firewater. Heap worse," said the Indian.

"Can't be anything worse than whisky," declared Cowboy Jack emphatically.

"Bad spirits," said the Indian stubbornly. "In box. Make knocking. White chief come see—come hear."

He called Cowboy Jack a "chief" because the white man owned the big ranch. Rose and Russ listened very earnestly to what the Indian said, and they urged Cowboy Jack to go to the Indian encampment and see what it meant.

"What's a spirit, Russ?" asked his sister.

"Alcohol," declared Russ, proud of his knowledge. "But I don't see how alcohol could knock on a box. It's a liquid—like water, you know."

They trotted after Cowboy Jack and the old Indian and came to the big box that had been locked in preparation for shipping back to the reservation when the Indians got through their job here with the picture company. It looked to be a perfectly innocent box, and at first the children and Cowboy Jack heard nothing remarkable from within it.

"I reckon you were hearing things in your mind, old fellow," said the ranchman to the Indian.

The latter grunted suddenly and pointed to the box. There was a sound that seemed to come from inside. Something made a rat, tat, tat on the cover of the box.

"Goodness me!" murmured Rose, quite startled.

"That's a real knocking," admitted Russ.

Cowboy Jack sprang forward and tried to open the box.

"Hey!" he exclaimed. "It's locked. Where's the key? When did you lock this box?"

"Black Bear—him lock it. Got key," said the old Indian, keeping well away from the box.

"You go and get that key in a hurry. Somebody is in that box, sure as you live!" cried the ranchman.

"I know! I know!" shouted Russ excitedly. "It's Mun Bun! They have locked him in that box!"

"Oh, poor little Mun Bun!" wailed Rose. "Do—do you suppose the Indians were trying to steal him?"

"Of course not," returned Russ disdainfully. "Mr. Black Bear wouldn't steal anybody. He just didn't know Mun Bun was in there. I guess Mun Bun crawled in by himself."

Then he went close to the big box and shouted Mun Bun's name, and they all heard the little boy reply—but his voice came to them very faintly.

"We'd better get him out in a hurry," said Cowboy Jack anxiously. "The little fellow might easily smother inside that box."

CHAPTER XXV

SOMETHING THAT WAS NOT EXPECTED

There was great excitement at the Indian camp during the next few minutes. Everybody came running to the spot when they heard that Mun Bun was found but could not be got at. Everybody but Chief Black Bear. He had gone off to a place at some distance from the camp, and a man on pony-back had to go to get him, for Black Bear had the key of the big box.

Daddy Bunker and mother came with the other Bunker children, and Vi began to ask questions as usual. But nobody paid much attention to her questions. Laddie said he thought he could make up a riddle about Mun Bun in the box, but before he managed to do this the chief arrived with the key.

When the lid of the box was lifted the first person Mun Bun saw was Daddy Bunker, and he put up his arms to him and cried:

"Daddy! Daddy! Mun Bun don't want to stay in this place. Mun Bun wants to go home."

"And I must say," said Mother Bunker, who had been much worried, "that home will be the very best place in the world after this. I will not let Mun Bun out of my reach again. How does he manage to get into so much trouble?"

"Why, Muvver!" sobbed the littlest Bunker, "I just tumble in. I tumbled into this box and then they locked me in."

"How does he tumble into trouble?" demanded Vi, staring at Mun Bun.

"I know there is a riddle about it," said Laddie thoughtfully. "Only I can't just make it out yet."

They were all very glad that Mun Bun was not hurt. But it did seem that he would have to be watched very closely or he might disappear again.

"He's just like a drop of quicksilver," said Cowboy Jack. "When you try to put your finger on him, he isn't there."

Just then the great horn blew to call everybody to the fort, for Mr. Habback was ready for the big scene of the picture. The little Bunkers—at least, all but Mun Bun—were eager to respond, for they wanted to be in the picture. Mother, however, kept the little boy with her, and they only watched the picture when it was made. That satisfied Mun Bun just as well, for he did not believe that he looked nice enough to go to a photographer just then.

"I guess I'll have my picture taken when I get back to Pineville, Muvver," he said. "I'll like it better."

But the rest of the party would never forget that exciting day. The Indians led by Black Bear attacked the fort, and there was much shooting and shouting and riding back and forth. The shooting was with blank cartridges, of course, so that nobody was hurt.

But even the ponies seemed to be excited, and Russ told Rose he was quite sure Pinky and his pinto, who were both in the picture, enjoyed the play just as much as anybody!

"Only, they will never see the picture when it is on the screen. And daddy says we will, if nothing happens. When the picture comes to Pineville we can take all the children we know at school and show 'em how we worked for the picture company and helped make 'A Romance of the Santa Fé Trail!'"

This, later, they did. But, of course, you will have to read about that in another story about the Six Little Bunkers.

Mr. Habback thanked the Bunkers when the work was done, and in the middle of the afternoon Cowboy Jack took them all back to the ranch house again in his big blue car, one of his cowboys leading in Pinky and the pinto pony later.

On the way to the ranch Russ and Rose heard daddy tell mother that he had managed to fix up Mr. Golden's business for him and that it would soon be time to start East.

"I don't care—much," Rose said, when she heard this. "We have had a very exciting time, Russ. And I guess I want to go to school again. They must have coal in Pineville. I should think they would have some by now."

"I hate to lose my pinto pony," said Russ.

"Can't we take him and Pinky with us?" Laddie asked. "I do wish we could."

"Can't do that," said daddy seriously. "We have enough pets now for Jerry Simms to look after."

"I tell you what," said Cowboy Jack heartily. "I'll take good care of the ponies, little folks, so that when you come out to see me again they will be all ready for you to use."

"And Jerry, too?" cried Mun Bun. "I like that pony. He doesn't run so fast."

"And Jerry, too," agreed the ranchman.

So the little Bunkers were contented with this promise.

When they got to the ranch house everybody there seemed very glad to see them, and Maria, the Mexican cook, had a very nice supper ready for the six little Bunkers. She seemed to know that she would not cook for the visitors much longer, and she tried to please them particularly with this meal. There were waffles again, and all the little Bunkers were fond of those delectable dainties. Only Mother Bunker would not always let them eat as many as they wanted to.

But there was something at the ranch besides supper that evening that interested the children very much. There was some more mail from the East, and among it a little package that had been registered and sent to Mother Bunker by Captain Ben from Grand View.

"I guess he has sent Mother Bunker a nice present," declared Rose eagerly. "Captain Ben likes mother."

"Don't we all like her?" demanded Vi. "I like her very much. Can't I give her a present too?"

"You are always picking flowers and finding pretty things for me," said Mrs. Bunker kindly. "I appreciate them just as much as any present Captain Ben could give me."

"But what is it, Mother?" asked Rose, quite as excited as Vi and the others.

"We shall have to open it and see," her mother said.

But she would not open the little package until after supper. Perhaps that is why the little Bunkers were willing to eat fewer of Maria's nice waffles. They were all eager to see what was in the package. Even daddy claimed to be curious.

So, when the lamps were lit in the big living room and everybody was more than ready, as Russ complained, Mother Bunker began to untie the string which fastened the package from Captain Ben.

"I guess it is a diamond necklace," declared Rose earnestly.

"Oh, maybe it is a pretty pearl brooch," said Russ.

"What do you suppose it is, Daddy?" asked Mother Bunker, busy with the string and seals and smiling at Mr. Bunker knowingly.

"It isn't a white elephant, I am sure," chuckled Daddy Bunker.

"Oh! Now he is making fun," cried Rose. "It is something pretty, of course, for mother."

"I know! I know!" cried Laddie suddenly. "I know what it is."

"If you know so much," returned his twin "tell us."

"It's a riddle," declared Laddie.

"I guess it must be," laughed his mother. "'Riddle-me-ree! What do I see?'" and she opened the outside wrapper and displayed a little box with a letter wrapped about it.

"From Captain Ben to be sure," she said, unfolding the letter and beginning to read it.

"And it is a riddle!" repeated Laddie with conviction.

Mother Bunker began to laugh. She nodded and smiled at them.

"It certainly is a riddle," she said. "It is almost as good a riddle as that one Laddie told about the splinter."

"I know! I know!" cried the little boy. "'I went out to the woodpile and got it.' I remember that one. But—but that isn't a splinter he has sent you, is it, Mother?"

"It is something that Captain Ben looked for and could not find. But all the time he had it. What is it?"

The little Bunkers stared at each other. Laddie murmured:

"That is a riddle! What can it be?"

Suddenly Rose uttered a little squeal and clasped her hands.

"Oh, Mother!" she cried. "Is it—is it my watch?"

At that Laddie began fairly to dance up and down. He was so excited he could scarcely speak.

"Is it my pin?" he wanted to know. "My stick-pin that I left at Grand View, Mother? Is it?"

There certainly was great excitement in the room until Mother Bunker opened the box. And there lay in cotton-wool the missing watch and stick-pin. Captain Ben had hunted a second time for the lost treasures the little Bunkers had so carelessly left behind, and had found the watch and pin.

Rose and Laddie were so delighted that they could only laugh and dance about for a few minutes. But Vi was rather disappointed that it was not, after all, a present for Mother Bunker.

It was quite late before the little Bunkers could get settled in their beds that night. That is, all but Mun Bun. He fell asleep in Mother Bunker's lap and did not know much about what went on.

Rose and Laddie promised not to lose their treasures again. And, of course, they had not meant to leave the watch and pin behind at Grand View. But daddy told them that thoughtlessness always bred trouble and disappointment.

"Like Mun Bun getting into the Indian's trunk," said Vi seriously. "He made us a lot of trouble to-day."

Mun Bun made them no more trouble while they remained on the ranch, for Mother Bunker and Rose were especially careful in watching him. The little boy did not mean to get lost; but Cowboy Jack laughingly said that Mun Bun seemed to have that habit.

"Some day you folks are going to mislay that boy and won't find him so easily. I tell you, he is a regular drop of quicksilver."

But after that, although the six little Bunkers had plenty of fun at Cowboy Jack's, they had no dangerous adventure. They rode and drove the ponies, and played with the dogs, and watched the cowboys herd the cattle and some of the men train horses to saddle-work that had never been ridden before and did not seem to like the idea at all of carrying people on their backs.

"It is lucky Pinky and your calico pony don't mind carrying us," Laddie remarked on one occasion to Russ. "I guess if they pitched like those big horses do, they would throw us right over their heads on to the ground."

"Well, my pinto threw me once," said Russ rather proudly. "But it only shook me up a little. And, of course, accidents are apt to happen anywhere and to anybody."

But Laddie did not think he would care to be thrown over Pinky's head. Rose had told him it was not a nice experience at all!

In a few days the Bunkers packed their trunks and bags and the big blue automobiles came around to the door, and they bade everybody at Cowboy Jack's ranch good-bye. They had had a lovely time—all of them.

"And I've had the best time of all having you here," declared the ranchman. "I hate to have you little Bunkers go. I don't see, Charlie, why you can't spare two or three of them and let 'em stay with me."

"I guess not!" exclaimed Daddy Bunker. "We have just enough children. We couldn't really stand another one, but we can't spare one of these we have. Could we, Mother?"

Mother Bunker quite agreed. She "counted noses" when the six little Bunkers were packed into the cars with the baggage. You see, after all, it was quite a task to keep account of so many children at one time. And especially if they chanced to be as lively as were the six little Bunkers, who never remained—any of them—in one spot for long at a time. That made them particularly hard to count.

Russ and Rose and Laddie and Violet and Margy and Mun Bun all told Cowboy Jack that they had had a good time, and they hoped to see him again. If they do ever go to Cowboy Jack's ranch again I hope I shall know about it. And if I do, I will surely tell you all that happens to the Six Little Bunkers.

THE END

Milton Keynes UK
Ingram Content Group UK Ltd.
UKHW050207070724
445042UK00012B/543

9 781836 573357